Were Chronicles

PACK ROGUE

CRISSY SMITH

Dedication

For my family, whom I love and cherish even through the
tough times.

Books by Crissy Smith

Pack Rogue

ISBN # 978-1-78686-133-7

©Copyright Crissy Smith 2017

Cover Art by Posh Gosh ©Copyright 2017

Interior text design by Claire Siemaszkiewicz

Totally Bound Publishing

Published in 2017 by Totally Bound Publishing, Newland House, The Point, Weaver Road, Lincoln, LN6 3QN, United Kingdom.

Chapter One

Kiley Palmer sat scrunched down inside her SUV, well-hidden by the tinted windows as she held up a camera and snapped pictures. The old man had been right. The fourth Mrs. Douglas had a visitor every morning when her husband left for work. Of course, Kiley had already known the woman was guilty. The first night after Kiley had been hired, she'd shifted into her wolf form and stalked the area.

The scents of the humans who came and went from the house hadn't been numerous and she hadn't been able to separate the older gentleman's smell from other male odors easily. But she'd still had to get photographic proof for her client, since she couldn't actually convince a human her nose told her the guy's wife was cheating.

Maybe if the shifters went public like the Council wanted, she would be able to use one of her enhanced senses as evidence, but until then, she had to do things the old-fashioned way. So, she'd been stuck inside her vehicle, watching like a peeping Tom until she'd finally gotten the chance to use her camera.

"Gotcha," she whispered to empty air, clicking four more pictures before the front door of the large house closed.

How stupid could this woman be? Not only did she kiss her lover in broad daylight, but he'd only waited ten minutes after the husband had left before he'd shown up. What if Mr. Douglas had been running late?

It might be possible the young man didn't realize the woman he was sleeping with was married, but Kiley doubted it. She'd peeked inside the windows and seen the pictures of the couple.

Disgust made her stomach roll. She'd grown used to seeing spouses cheating by now, but Kiley really hated these cases. However, over sixty percent of her work centered around some sort of infidelity.

What Kiley really wanted to do full-time was the investigations that led her to reconnecting families. Those were the circumstances Kiley enjoyed. A bare month ago, she'd found a young man who'd moved away from his family and had disappeared right after his eighteenth birthday. The young man, Adam, had run scared because of his sexual orientation. Certain his family would disown him, he had left them before he'd be kicked out.

His mom and dad had been frightened and desperate. When Kiley had gotten the call for help, she'd put aside another cheating spouse job to locate their son.

She'd found him. Living in a small apartment without heat and food, struggling to get by. He'd cried when Kiley had told him his parents wanted him to come home. Adam had refused, confessing why he'd left in the first place. Since Adam's mom had already told Kiley the reason she believed he'd run, Kiley had known that the kid's parents only wanted him safe. She'd put Adam on the phone with his mom and even though she'd tried to give them privacy, she'd heard both sides of the conversation.

The sobbing, apologies and heartfelt loving words had had her tearing up, too. She would never have a family reunion like that, but at least she'd gotten to witness something beautiful.

She'd dropped Adam off at his parents' house an hour after she'd located him.

Kiley still smiled every time she thought about that family's happy ending. She hadn't wanted to charge the parents, but she had a living to make, so she'd given them a price of half of what she normally made.

Mr. Douglas' situation would help pay the rest of her bills this month, anyway. He had enough money to pay her full rate and then some.

She tipped back her head and closed her eyes, knowing she had plenty of time until Mrs. Douglas would be done with her lover. She squirmed a little in her seat, trying to get comfortable. Spring had finally come, warming up the afternoons, but the morning air still held a chill. Kiley hated being cold. She knew it was because of her childhood, but she couldn't help it. She often thought about moving someplace where it never grew cold, like Arizona, but she hadn't gotten up the nerve to seriously consider it. Here, she was safe. The Alpha of the local Pack didn't expect too much of her and Kiley hardly ever had trouble with other shifters. Kiley might have been an anomaly when it came to wolf shifters, but she had to watch out for herself.

Fuck, she didn't want her thoughts to go down that road. Kiley was happy in her little world and rarely let herself dwell on her past. She wouldn't do it now.

Kiley reached for her coffee and found the cup empty. *Damn*, she thought, sitting back with a sigh. She contemplated running to the closest convenience store to grab another cup when a knock on the passenger window startled her.

She jumped, bringing her hand to her heart. The grin from the man on the other side of the glass annoyed and amused her at the same time.

It seemed her thoughts had conjured the man. She rolled down her window while scowling at the good-looking shifter. "Detective," she greeted.

Detective Gray Mason continued to grin as he leaned against her door. He ran his gaze over her slowly and Kiley almost blushed. It was a very appraising look and made her hot.

"How's it going?" he finally asked.

Kiley shrugged. She ignored the pulse of heat that flared between them. "Fine, until you scared the living daylights out of me." She made sure to glare at him, although she didn't mean it. She liked Gray, even when he annoyed her.

He chuckled in response. "I thought you might be sleeping

on the job."

Kiley crossed her arms over her chest and gave him her best pout. "So you also thought giving me a heart attack would be okay?"

Unfazed, he continued to smile. "All done here?" he asked.

Kiley looked at the house and then at him. With Gray turning serious, she knew it wasn't so much a question as him telling her she was done. She nodded, because she knew she couldn't say no.

He opened her door and held out a hand. "I need you to come with me."

She rolled her shoulders and climbed from her vehicle, ignoring his offer of help. He stepped aside, giving her room as another man moved forward, drawing her attention. Kiley frowned at the guard. She didn't know Wyatt well, but he had a reputation for being a hardcore fighter. Gray finding her wasn't unusual, but he normally came alone when he collected her.

"What's going on?" she asked Gray, snapping her gaze from one man to the other. Dread scrawled up her spine and unease settled in her stomach. This couldn't be good.

"He needs to see you," Gray told her quietly. "At the house."

Kiley shook her head and backed toward her SUV. "No." She knew what this weekend was about. She'd seen the many cars which had driven through town on their way up to the compound. The gathering of Alphas to discuss Council business ensured she would be nowhere near the local Pack.

Gray's hand on her elbow stopped her. "It'll be okay. I'll stay with you," he promised.

Of course Gray knew exactly how she felt. He was one of the few people who knew why she refused to join the Pack. Kiley hated being called a Rogue, but never would she ever put herself in the hands of another. No—she was responsible for herself and no one else got to make decisions concerning her.

"It's important," Gray said. "Please."

The *please* almost got her. Kiley's heart sank. She hated to refuse but couldn't be anywhere near the compound with so many dominant male wolves. She'd do anything else for the Alpha who gave her the space she needed while not pressuring her to commit to the Pack. She and Tyler had an understanding and she didn't want to disappoint or anger him.

"Come on," Gray urged with a gentle tug.

Kiley tried to plant her feet. "I'll follow you."

Gray shook his head. "I don't think so," he quipped.

Kiley bit her bottom lip. Damn, she'd already used that trick.

"Wyatt will drive your vehicle and follow," Gray explained. "You won't be without a way home."

Kiley knew she should be grateful. At least they were giving her a way out without depending on one of the Pack members. It was a small thing, but it made her relax a little, just as Gray had probably known it would. In the year the man had lived in her city, he had gotten to know her better than anyone else. Sometimes she hated that fact, like right then.

One foot in front of the other, she let Gray lead her to the big Hummer parked behind her SUV.

"This new?" she inquired. It had to be, since she'd never seen it before — damn, it was huge.

Gray shrugged and she grinned.

"Over-compensating much?" she teased.

Gray growled, opening the passenger door. "Get in."

Kiley giggled. "Oh, yes, sir," she said innocently, teasing Gray, which relaxed her. It had, after all, become one of her favorite activities.

Gray's lips twitched as if he fought a smile. Kiley had settled in the seat and pulled her seat belt on by the time he'd made it to the driver's door and gotten in. She glanced at him out of the corner of her eye.

Gray was one of the few Pack members she would actually call a friend. A police detective, he matched her ideal of the perfect strong male. He was well built. The play of muscles under his dress shirt, the wide shoulders and the plain bulk of the man both intimidated and aroused her. His kind heart and quick wit were added bonuses.

There had been numerous times in the past she had wished she'd fall in love with him. They'd fooled around a few times, but as good as it had been, it hadn't been what either of them were looking for. They were not destined to be mates. Which saddened her. She had never expected to be given the chance to find her mate. At one time, it had been forbidden, in fact. She had already been spoken for, or she had been until her Alpha had finally come across someone he couldn't threaten or beat into submission.

Lost in her thoughts, she hadn't realized they'd started to move until Gray reached over and intertwined his fingers with hers. Kiley leaned back her head and closed her eyes.

"What does he want to see me for?"

Since the night she had been released from her own living Hell, she had tried to avoid contact with other shifters. Especially any Alpha. Tyler was okay, but he kept his distance. His daughter, Jesse, was what they had in common. Kiley loved Jesse and had babysat the young girl several times. Tyler wanted Jesse to have a strong female influence and it brought Kiley to the compound, so he could check on her. Kiley knew Tyler could get anyone from his Pack to watch the child, but she really liked the job.

Gray lifted Kiley's palm to his face and ran his cheek over her knuckles before kissing the back of her hand. "I believe he has a job for you."

Kiley began to get lost in the sensations Gray caused. She shivered as her body instantly heated. They might never be mates, but Gray still aroused her. "A job?" she breathed.

"There have been threats."

Kiley blinked in surprise, pulling away to concentrate. "Threats? Against who? Tyler? Oh, my God, Jesse!"

"Yes," Gray said with a frown. "The danger is to anyone who agrees to come out publicly. All Council members and Alphas."

How horrible. While Kiley didn't understand the need for the shifters to become public, there was no way she'd allow anyone to hurt the sweet Jesse. But even though she enjoyed watching over the girl, Tyler had enough guards to protect Jesse and the rest of the Pack. "Why does he need me?"

"Always so suspicious," Gray commented.

Kiley grunted but didn't reply.

Gray's heavy sigh sounded loudly through the vehicle. "It's complicated."

Kiley nodded, even though he wasn't looking at her. *Fine.* So Gray couldn't tell her. Meaning the Alpha had to be the one to do that.

Tyler might be lax with her, but rules were rules. And from everything she knew about Gray, he followed Tyler's orders. Always.

Hell, Gray had moved across the country behind Tyler when the Council had asked Tyler to take over the broken Pack Riker had left behind.

Had it only been a year since the new Alpha had come to Clear Water, Colorado? It seemed so long ago. In a matter of hours, her life had changed. Her Pack leader had been run off and now Tyler led.

Riker had been the Alpha who had led during her entire life.

Her entire tormented life.

Kiley didn't know the other members of the Pack. By the time Riker had had control of her, she'd been separated from the Pack by her father. Too many bad memories had overshadowed the few from her childhood. There were some names she remembered, but she had never given them a thought once Riker had her. Lost and living in misery, Kiley had only tried to survive. Until the day the cellar door had opened and Tyler had stomped down the stairs.

She didn't know who had been more shocked. Her or

Tyler.

Tyler had almost fallen when he'd spotted her chained in the corner.

Kiley hadn't known if Tyler was one of the men who Riker had brought by once in a while to use and abuse her, so she'd bared her teeth in warning.

Tyler had crouched down and made soothing sounds until he'd gotten close enough to release her. Kiley had been locked up for so long that even when the big, thick chains had been taken off, she hadn't moved. God, she could still see the pity in Tyler's gaze when he'd reached for her.

"Hey, you okay?"

Gray's deep voice startled her from her memories.

"Sure," she said quietly, rubbing her upper arms. She was so cold, like she'd been in that hellhole.

"Tyler will take care of you," Gray said. "You should realize that."

"Yeah," Kiley said. She didn't know what else to add. Tyler was a good Alpha and she trusted him as much as she trusted anyone. Which wasn't a lot.

At least Tyler hadn't pressured her into joining his Pack. He hadn't pressured anyone. Most of the Pack had left and joined other established Packs before Tyler had even shown up. Kiley had heard some had returned, wanting to be back in their homes, but since Kiley had never met them, she didn't care. They hadn't even been aware of her existence.

Tyler had brought his own people with him, mixing her old Pack into a new one. The Pack grew even now. Kiley kept an eye out for new residents in town and for rumors that had to do with the local Pack. The city didn't belong to shifters alone, but knowing the right people, Kiley heard what the Pack was up to.

She used the knowledge as a way to protect herself. Kiley wanted to watch those around her so she had advance warning if she needed to run. Or stay away from the Alpha compound like she'd wanted to do the upcoming weekend.

The meeting between Alphas to discuss going public was

a big deal. Tyler had told her himself what the weekend meant, understanding she'd be nervous with all the guests showing up.

Tyler was thoughtful like that. He knew what she had gone through and, even if she didn't belong to him or his Pack, he watched out for her. For that reason alone, Kiley vowed to help in any way possible.

As they left the city behind for the secluded woods where the Alpha's home stood, tension invaded her body. Too many memories haunted her for Kiley to be able to control her fear.

As if he could feel Kiley's growing nervousness, Gray smiled over at her. "We took some of the pups for their first shift this past weekend," he told her.

"Really?" Kiley turned to lean against the door so she could see Gray better. "How'd that go?" It was nerve-racking the first time a newbie shifted with the Pack. Kiley still remembered the sickness she'd felt as she'd stared at the other kids her age when it had been her time.

The tradition of the Packs was for the high-ranking members to take the teenagers into the woods to spend time with them and show them the easiest way to call forward their wolf. Usually there was some sort of funny story or unexpected crisis that popped up.

"So Wyatt is working with Dean Johnson," Gray began. "You remember Dean from Jesse's birthday?"

"Yeah." She recalled the skinny red-headed boy who'd spent most of the gathering under a tree, reading. "Quiet kid."

Gray snorted. "Well, he wasn't very quiet when Wyatt was giving him instructions on how to picture his wolf to bring forward the animal—and he only managed to shift his paws and tail. The boy was jumping around screeching and yelling."

"Oh, my God!" Kiley managed in between gales of laughter.

Gray was also chuckling. "Wyatt's trying to get a hold

of Dean to calm him enough to finish the transformation, but Dean's jumping around in a panic. Wyatt tripped and ended up with a face full of dirt."

That made Kiley laugh even harder, thinking about the stoic man who was driving her vehicle at that moment.

"Dean starts bumping into the other teens, who are freaked out seeing their buddy in a partial shift," Gray continued. "The smaller other pups begin to refuse to even try the change."

"That...that's terrible," Kiley got out.

"Wyatt's there yelling for some help, but the other guards are falling all over one another, laughing so hard they can't assist Wyatt at all."

"Oh, my God!" Kiley repeated. She could actually picture the scene that Gray was describing. "Wait." She grabbed his hand. "You were there. What were you doing?"

"Trying not to piss myself," Gray stated with amusement. "It was fucking hilarious."

Kiley rolled her eyes, although she didn't know if she'd have been any more help than Gray seemingly hadn't been. "And?"

"Wyatt stands up and stalks toward Dean, who has his back to Wyatt as he's shrieking. I managed to grasp Dean's shoulders to try to get him to quiet down and listen. Which wasn't working."

"I bet it wasn't," she agreed. Kiley couldn't even imagine how terrified Dean must have felt. While she was amused by the story, it had to have been mortifying for the poor teen.

"Anyway, I'm distracting Dean and Wyatt comes up behind him. I turn Dean around and Wyatt leaps at him with his canines lengthened. Dean screams in terror and finally, *finally* shifts completely."

"That's good," Kiley praised. They had gotten the kid to transform.

"Except for the fact that Dean took off at full speed," Gray informed her. "None of us had transformed yet, so we couldn't catch him."

"Oh, no!" Kiley said after gasping.

"It took two fucking hours to hunt him down, since he didn't know where he was going and kept backtracking and going in circles."

"But you found him?"

Gray nodded. "He'd fallen asleep on top of the slide at the playground."

By this time, they'd reached the outside of the stone gates barring the road that led to the Alpha house and she wiped tears of laughter from her eyes. "That's great."

"It was an eventful night," Gray said. "But I made Tyler promise not to put me on that detail again for at least six months. I was exhausted and slept for twenty-four hours straight after that."

Kiley started to tease him about getting old, but a young, handsome guard waved Gray inside once the barrier slowly opened. All amusement fled. Kiley gripped the seat as she tried to calm her racing heart.

"Breathe, Kiley," Gray urged quietly, driving toward the big house.

She took a deep breath and counted to ten. Several unknown vehicles were stationed there and she took stock of each one. She liked to be prepared in case she needed to make a quick exit. If one of these vehicles followed her, she would know. Several yards from the compound, she saw a new house in the process of being constructed.

The beautiful brickwork and large glass windows looked welcoming and secure at the same time.

"What's that?" she asked Gray, with a nod to the building.

"Tyler's having a new main house built."

"Really?" Kiley asked, shocked. The compound was big and solid. It had been a point of pride for Riker and had cost the Pack a lot of money. She hated it but thought that was where an Alpha belonged.

"He hates the compound. Says it's like living in a tomb. He wants a happy place to raise the cubs and welcome the

Pack," Gray informed her. "He's taking suggestions on what to do with it. He doesn't want to waste the building because of the expense, but he's thinking about making it into a school or community center for the Pack. He wants the compound to belong to everyone."

"Wow!" Kiley couldn't help the awe in her voice. *What a great idea.* Giving the compound over to the Pack would sure erase some of the evil deeds that had been done inside the building. Plus, she wouldn't mind spending more time with Jesse if she didn't have to visit where she'd been held captive.

Gray turned in his seat after he'd cut the engine. He slipped his arm behind her neck and she leaned in to his touch. It felt good, knowing Gray cared for her. He might not be in love with her, but the affection was obvious.

"Maybe I can take you out to dinner after this?" he inquired.

It had been a few months since they'd been together and Kiley was more than ready to reconnect with him. Even if they would never be mates, she still had strong feelings for the man.

"I'd like that," she agreed. No reason not to enjoy him, especially after finding out whatever Tyler wanted to tell her.

He smiled at her once more, his eyes warm and inviting as he reached for the door handle on his side. "Well, then, let's get this party started so we can get to the good stuff."

Kiley shook her head, grinning, following his lead and climbing from the monster vehicle. She had to jump to get down. The front door opened ahead of them reaching it and Kiley barely had enough time to brace herself before her arms were full of a small six-year-old girl.

"Daddy said you were coming!" Jesse squealed, hugging Kiley's neck tight.

Kiley patted the little cub. "Hey, sunshine, miss me?"

"Uh-huh." Jesse nodded excitedly. "I've been waiting for hours!"

Gray chuckled, pressing his hand against the small of Kiley's back, urging her forward. "It didn't take that long."

Jesse rolled her eyes as only a young child could. "Seemed like it to me."

"I tried to tell Gray to hurry," Kiley teased. "But you know cops. They gotta obey all the rules."

Gray growled playfully, but the two females ignored him.

"Yeah, he never goes fast. Not like Dominic," Jesse whispered.

Dominic Adams, the Alpha's Beta and brother, stepped out from the shadows at the mention of his name. "Are you telling my secrets?" he asked Jesse, winking at Kiley.

Jesse clapped a hand over her mouth and shook her head. Everyone laughed at her antics.

"Come now." Dominic held out his arms for Jesse. "Let Kiley see your daddy and then you can hang all over her."

Bright, innocent eyes looked up at Kiley. "Promise?"

Immediately, guilt flooded Kiley. She didn't see Jesse enough. The young girl had attached herself to Kiley on her first visit. There was nothing like the heart-melting feeling of the total love the cub gave. Jesse had quickly become one of her favorite people in the world.

"I promise," she told Jesse with one last hug before she allowed Dominic to take her.

"They're waiting for the two of you in the study," he said with a more business-like tone than he'd used with Jesse.

Gray nodded and took Kiley's elbow to lead her. Kiley concentrated on remaining calm as they walked down the long hall. She'd been in Tyler's office more than a dozen times, but this was different. The entire compound buzzed with a stressful energy Kiley didn't know how to respond to.

Gray knocked on the door and they waited for the command to enter. Gray pushed the door open, Kiley remaining behind him. As she stepped into the room, she suddenly got hit by the strongest, most intoxicating scent. She gasped as her body responded quickly and she became light-headed. Gray blocked her view of the room, but even without looking, she knew she was in deep trouble.

She didn't need to see the man to know Austin Winters waited inside.

Austin Winters snapped his head up a moment prior to the knock sounding on the study door. By the time it opened, he'd risen to his feet. Kiley's scent hit him hard and he'd taken a step forward the second she entered. He couldn't see her, but the gasp of breath and the overwhelming emotions he felt combined to almost make his knees buckle. His Beta and best friend, Colt, grabbed his arm.

The room remained silent, the others recognizing the strong aroma of attraction that flowed from both him and Kiley. Oh, she knew he was there and the dominant part of him rose quickly, as well as the urge to claim what belonged to him. What he'd wanted since she'd walked away from the hotel room where they'd spent one glorious night together.

Austin didn't like that a man stood between him and Kiley. A growl reverberated deep in his throat and he couldn't hold it in. The man looked over at him with an expression that surprised Austin. Instead of fear of the Alpha, his look showed sympathy. He nodded and stepped to the side. Austin understood immediately. The expression on Kiley's face appeared panicked.

Austin took a step toward her, dislodging Colt's hand, his only thought to comfort her. Her eyes widened and she scrambled away. Austin paused, confused. She'd obviously recognized him, so shouldn't she be just as excited to see him as he was to have finally found her?

Tyler sighed before he cleared his throat. It proved tough to do, but Austin took his eyes off his mate and looked at the other Alpha.

"Austin, you've met Grayson, and this is Kiley Palmer," he introduced.

Austin didn't understand the currents shifting around

the room. Tyler was trying to convey something to him, but he wasn't picking it up. He wanted to cross the room and grab the woman who he'd thought he'd never see again. His fingers literally itched to touch her.

After hours of meetings and talking shit out, Kiley's arrival astonished him. It was a cause for celebration.

Tyler walked to him and clasped him on the shoulder. "Kiley, this is Austin Winters—a good friend of mine and Alpha of a Pack further south. But I'm guessing you already know that."

She nodded, mutely.

"She is very uneasy at being around any shifter, much less powerful ones," Tyler murmured quietly to Austin. "I'm not sure how the two of you know each other, but this doesn't need to take place in front of everyone in here. She's about to bolt."

Members of both his Pack and Tyler's filled the room. While the meeting had already started, the only thing he cared about was finding out what was wrong with Kiley. Austin wanted to snarl and demand they all got the hell away.

Luckily, Tyler was ahead of him and more diplomatic. "Gentlemen, if you'd please give us a minute. Grayson will take you to get a drink and I'm sure we have some snacks made in the kitchen."

As soon as everyone headed to the door, Kiley glanced at him. Her intent was clear and Austin tensed. He would chase her this time. He met her eyes squarely and tried to convey that to her. If she ran, he would follow.

"Kiley..." Tyler called in warning.

Her expression didn't change. She shifted on the balls of her feet.

"Kiley, I need to speak with you for a minute. I'll allow Tyler to stay with you if you'd like," Austin tried, speaking softly.

Confusion and doubt covered her face. She obviously wasn't sure about trusting him. The room had cleared out and Austin watched Gray gently push her farther into the room, closing the door behind him.

Terror began to set in the second she was alone with them, Austin noticed. Trying to put her at ease, Austin relaxed in the overstuffed chair he'd occupied earlier and gestured to the couch. "Would you like to have a seat?"

She watched him warily as she walked around the room so she wouldn't pass in front of him. Tyler, to his relief, stood behind him, giving him the opportunity to address only her. He didn't know Kiley well, but her behavior seemed so different from the night they'd met that Austin had a hard time deciding what to say.

She sat. Too far away, in his opinion, but at least she did face him.

"It's good to see you again," he began.

She shook her head. "Wh...what are you doing here?"

Austin leaned forward. "We'll get into that shortly," he told her. "I wasn't aware you were a member of Tyler's Pack."

"I'm not."

He waited for her to continue, but when she didn't, he glanced over his shoulder at Tyler.

"It's complicated," Tyler said softly.

Must be, because Austin was picking up all kinds of conflicting emotions from both his friend and Kiley. Jesus, were her and Tyler an item? Had Austin slept with a woman who his buddy had a claim to? Horror filled him as he stared at Tyler.

"It's not whatever you're thinking," Tyler said. "Kiley isn't a member of my Pack, but she does watch Jesse for me often. We're...friends."

She snorted, but Austin kept his gaze on Tyler.

"Kiley lives in town, but she doesn't belong to my Pack," Tyler said slowly.

Austin knew he'd missed something important. Tyler was trying to convey a message, but Austin wasn't getting it.

"I'm Rogue," Kiley practically shouted.

He whipped his head around to stare at her. A female wolf shifter who was Rogue? Austin had never heard of such a thing. The women shifters were to be cherished and protected at all costs.

"Okay," Austin said gently.

Kiley laughed. "That's all you have to say?"

He shrugged. "I have no clue what to say about that. I don't really know you, now, do I? You made sure of that when you snuck out of my bed in the middle of the night."

Tyler coughed while Kiley blushed. Austin enjoyed seeing the light pink tint to her face and neck. It reminded him of how she'd looked sated from pleasure.

"I didn't realize you were an Alpha," Kiley said quietly.

Austin didn't understand how she'd missed that fact. Not only did his dominance radiate from him, but it had also seemed to turn her on. "Really?" he asked in disbelief.

She shrugged. "I don't know you that well, now, do I?"

She might have repeated his words to him, but Austin wasn't buying her flippant attitude.

"Better than most other shifters," he replied. "Even if you didn't stick around to learn more."

Kiley pressed her lips together while narrowing her eyes. "We had a one-night stand," she spat. "Get over it. Hundreds of men and women a month do so."

"We didn't have a one-night stand," Austin corrected. "That was just the first night out of many, many more we'll enjoy."

She jerked, staring at him in shock. Pleased with her reaction, Austin secretly enjoyed it. He was putting his feelings out in the open, with an audience no less, but he didn't have a choice. He'd been pissed off ever since he'd let her get away.

Never in his life had he experienced what he had with Kiley. If she'd still been in his bed when he'd woken, Austin would have dragged her to his house and never let her go. He'd been heartbroken and devastated, finding Kiley nowhere in the hotel room.

"You..." Kiley pointed at him. "You can't..."

"Yes, I can," he interrupted. "I'm telling you now I have no intention of letting you run from me again."

"You don't have a choice," she said, but Kiley squirmed in her seat, looking at him.

That was how she'd acted previously, so he finally knew how to deal with her. Kiley had been begging for an Alpha to make her feel safe. She might not be aware of how she came across to him, but Austin sensed it, and that was all that mattered.

"Look at me, Kiley," he demanded.

She raised her head.

"It's going to be okay," he promised. "We have time to work all this out and no one is going to pressure you to accept anything you don't want." Austin had to choose his words carefully. He wouldn't break a promise to her, but Austin had every intention of claiming her eventually.

"Uh, okay."

He nodded in approval. Fuck, he wanted to pull her into his lap and comfort her, but Kiley wasn't ready for that as long as they had an audience. He'd have to save it for later, when they were alone.

"Tyler?" He motioned for his friend to take over the conversation. Austin had known the Alpha had called in help to protect Jesse, but he'd had no idea the help would be coming from the woman he dreamt about. *Huh. Funny the way fate works.* Two months ago, he'd met the most perfect woman in the world and now she'd just dropped right in his lap.

"Kiley, I asked you to the house because I need a favor." Tyler moved closer to her as he spoke.

She nodded. "Gray said you had a job for me."

Austin bit back a growl at the casual way she said Tyler's Enforcer's name. She remained wary of him—a lover—while she spoke the other man's name naturally. Austin wondered how close they were. The wolf inside him grew agitated, so he took several deep breaths to calm himself while Tyler continued to talk.

"I have a few guests coming to speak with Austin and myself about the Council decision to go public. I told you about this."

"Yes," Kiley agreed.

"It's been planned for several months."

Austin watched Kiley take in the information. He could practically see the wheels turning in her head, trying to work out what Tyler needed.

"We've received several anonymous calls, starting as soon as the meetings were set. Austin was already planning to come down to be in the talks with us, and he also got threatening phone calls," Tyler told her.

Kiley glanced over at him and he sent her a reassuring smile.

She nodded and gave her attention to Tyler.

"I can't *not* have the summits. It doesn't matter if we choose to go public or not, I cannot back down. It would put the entire Pack in danger," Tyler explained.

Kiley nodded. "Makes sense. What do you need from me?"

"Jesse," Tyler said simply.

"Oh, God!" Kiley exclaimed. "The threats aren't against her, are they?"

Tyler frowned. "They're against all of us. I can't take the chance of something happening to her."

"I'll do anything for Jesse, you know that."

Austin grinned. That boded well for their future together. He wanted cubs, lots and lots of cubs.

"I want you to stay here with her as her guard. You can spend time with her and keep her from getting worried and hopefully out of trouble."

"Yeah." Kiley laughed. "No problem there."

Tyler shook his head with a wide smile. "I know you'll try your best. So will you help?"

Kiley glanced over at him and he raised an eyebrow in

challenge. The question being, would Kiley put what had happened between them ahead of protecting an innocent child?

"I'll help," she agreed.

"Wonderful," Austin commented, standing. "And that will give us some time together, too." Austin thought of all the possibilities. It would be hard for Kiley to avoid him in the house, even though the huge compound had numerous rooms and hidey spots. It was true he had meetings to concentrate on, but nothing would keep him from getting to know her better. Fate had finally smiled down on him.

"Yeah."

She rose, too, and he wanted to laugh at the disbelief on her face.

Oh, she'd fight this, but Austin looked forward to the challenge. One taste hadn't been enough and by the way she ran her gaze down his body, Austin wondered how badly she wanted another taste of him, too.

"So." Kiley waved behind her. "I'll go find Jesse."

She turned and ran, fumbling with the door handle and eventually yanking it open. She was gone before he or Tyler could say another word.

Tyler sighed, drawing Austin's attention to his friend. Austin shook his head.

"It's a long story," Austin said.

"With Kiley, I have no doubt." Tyler strolled over and clapped him on the shoulder. "Please be careful. I don't want to see you hurt."

Austin frowned in confusion. He'd expected Tyler to tell him not to hurt *her*.

"I like Kiley," Tyler said. "She's a good person who's been through a lot. She won't hurt you on purpose, but she does have a tendency to run."

Yeah, Austin knew that.

"Even if she has feelings for you, Kiley won't be easy to tame."

Austin didn't want to tame her, though. He wanted Kiley

wild and strong. He'd had no idea she was Rogue and that scared him. A Rogue female didn't have the protection of Pack. "We'll both be okay," he said simply.

Tyler patted his shoulder. "I sure the hell hope so."

Tyler walked out of the office and Austin let him go. He knew there must be a story when it came to Kiley. He wouldn't ask Tyler, though. He wanted to hear it from Kiley.

Not ready to join the other shifters and restart the conference yet, Austin strolled over to the wide window to peer out over the backyard. Not far away, construction was still moving along. Austin rejoiced that Tyler had decided to build a new house. Austin couldn't have explained why he hated the large compound building, but he didn't feel at ease there.

Kiley stepped out onto the deck with Jesse's hand in hers, Jesse talking and jumping around while Kiley nodded. He stood there and watched them walking to the small play area beside the pool.

A few feet away from the swings, Jesse let go of Kiley's hand, racing ahead. Kiley laughed before chasing after the young pup. With his superior hearing and the window's thin glass, Austin picked up the sweet sound of Kiley's delight. She looked so different from the night they'd met. Oh, that night…

Inside the smoky bar, Kiley had been the most beautiful woman he'd ever seen. When Austin had arrived, to let off some steam, he'd expected to down a few drinks before going back to his lonely hotel room. Instead, he'd been immediately taken with the woman playing pool in the corner against a rather large scary-looking human.

From his seat at the bar, Austin had had the perfect view when Kiley had bent over the table to take her shot. Licking his lips, he could have practically tasted her even from across the room. He hadn't been the only one who'd noticed her, either.

When her game had ended and the human had stomped

off after being beaten by a girl, Kiley had peered around the room and their gazes had met. She'd jerked back a little, seemingly shocked by his presence. Austin still remembered the warmth that had spread through him, causing his cock to harden in his jeans. Her lips had twitched, telling him she'd noticed his reaction. Since he wasn't a man who wasted time or played games, he'd stalked across the room until he had stood in front of her. With every step he'd taken forward, she'd retreated until her back had been against the far wall.

Austin had caged her in with his arms stretched over her shoulders and his palms braced against the wall. Her intoxicating arousal had been enough for him to throw caution to the wind, kissing her hard and deep before a word had been spoken between them.

The way Kiley had reacted had literally taken his breath away. She'd been just as filled with need as he had. With their bodies brushing against each other's, it had been her idea to get out of the dingy establishment and find a place that was more private.

He'd grabbed her hand, towing her away from the other patrons and across the street to his room before she'd had time to change her mind. That fast, Austin had been sure she'd be unlike any lover he'd previously enjoyed. There'd been something about her that had spoken of true inner strength and he'd planned to find out every detail about her once they'd been sated.

Unfortunately, he hadn't had the chance, since, when he'd woken, Kiley had been gone.

Even as he'd blinked open his eyes that cold, early morning, Austin had been aware no one else had been present in the room.

Austin's heart actually ached and he rubbed his palm over his chest. He'd felt like a piece of him had disappeared along with her. Now, as he glimpsed her while she pushed Jesse on one of the swings, he was filled with renewed with hope. A chance to get back the feelings Kiley had brought out in him that night.

Her unexpected arrival made him doubt his own sanity, even. He'd been dreaming of her for so many months that he feared this was just another nighttime fantasy. He'd have to prove to himself she was really there. In the last place he'd expected.

Chapter Two

Kiley lifted Jesse into her arms and carried her airplane-style into the kitchen. Thanks to her wolf shifter abilities, she could easily hold the girl above her head without too much strain. Jesse giggled happily as they stepped through the open doorway, used to the shifters in her life being able to carry her.

The delighted sound warmed Kiley like nothing else had ever been able to do. She loved the little girl in her arms. The second they entered the kitchen, all conversation quieted. Kiley stopped short when her gaze fell on the men who occupied the space. She lowered Jesse to her side and wrapped her arm around the girl's shoulders — more for her benefit than Jesse's. Not having been paying close enough attention to her senses, she hadn't realized the men had taken a break from their early morning meeting.

Austin, Gray, Dominic and two other men sat around the large oak table. The men had looked over when they'd entered and all were smiling at them. Kiley shifted from foot to foot, trying to think of something to say. Anything that would take their attention from her and back to their breakfast. She couldn't resist seeking out Austin, though. Some part, deep down, wanted him to take control of the situation for her. Her gaze met his and he looked at her with such longing she had to glance quickly away. God, he was as attractive as she remembered. Remorse snuck in, but Kiley pushed it down where it belonged.

He'd been the only man she'd actually regretted having left in bed without a word. Even as the hotel room door had closed behind her that night, she'd had to fight to stop herself from turning around and going over to Austin. Their connection had been instant and while Kiley had known Austin was dominant, she'd never expected he'd be a fucking Alpha.

Even knowing what she did now, Kiley still wanted to go to him and drop to her knees so she could once again worship every inch of his body. She craved his touch.

It had been a long, stressful night and Kiley had barely managed to keep herself from seeking Austin's attention. Now it seemed she had run out of luck. Not only was he in the room with her, but so were a few others. Strangers — she hated strangers.

When she didn't say anything, Gray started to stand, a true friend who always seemed to know what she needed.

Austin growled, freezing the other man in place. Kiley glanced between the two. Tension poured from Austin. There'd be no way Austin could know about her past with Gray, so Kiley could only assume the Alpha was staking his claim. Kiley wanted to protest, but a bigger part of her felt pleased she'd attracted such a powerful male. *Damn shifter instincts.*

Gray looked unsure, while Austin had his teeth clenched. She had to do something prior to a fight breaking out or either man losing control of his wolf.

"It's okay," she whispered, knowing everyone would still be able to hear her. She didn't know who she was trying to reassure, though, her, Austin or Gray. She swallowed hard, then smiled. "Good morning," she greeted everyone, pretending the last few minutes hadn't happened.

Austin seemed to make an effort to relax and nodded. "Hello, ladies," he replied.

Kiley felt relieved that he'd played along. Shit, he was so perfect.

Jesse, who remained unaware of any tension, escaped from Kiley's hold and ran to her uncle. "Uncle Dom! Uncle Dom!"

The laughter in her voice seemed to spread until everyone

had a smile on their face.

"Yes?" Dominic answered the little girl.

"Kiley is going to stay the whole weekend with me!" Jesse bounced happily.

Dominic chuckled and lifted Jesse into his lap. "I heard that. What do you girls have planned?"

"Kiley said we'd make cookies!" Jesse squealed.

All eyes turned to her.

Kiley shrugged a shoulder. "It shouldn't be too hard."

Dominic and Gray groaned in unison.

"It's just cookies," Kiley growled in reply.

Dominic grinned at her, not saying anything.

Kiley glared then looked around the table. "I'm sure I can handle cookies."

"I'll be sure to keep the fire extinguisher handy," Gray quipped.

Austin and the two strangers didn't say anything, but Kiley could tell they were amused, too. She huffed out a breath and fisted her hands on her hips. "Oh, ha-ha," she muttered.

Austin stood and walked over to lay his arm around her shoulder. It took everything she had not to pull away. She got the feeling that he was once again staking his claim. She didn't want to embarrass Austin by denying him in front of the others, but he needed to realize Kiley was not the woman he should want. No way would she ever be part of his life in the way he needed, him being an Alpha.

"I'm sure you can do whatever you set your mind to."

The compliment from him came unexpectedly, but made her heart swell. She knew the others were only teasing her, but it felt good to have someone on her side for once. She found herself leaning in to Austin's embrace.

"Thank you," she whispered, for his ears only.

"Maybe I can even help," he offered. "I do know my way around the kitchen."

Before she could reply, Austin tightened his arm for a second then pulled her forward. "I'd like you to meet some people," he told her.

Kiley let him lead her over to the table where the men sat and Jesse happily swung her legs in her uncle's lap.

"Kiley, this is my Beta, Colt." He introduced an attractive blond man. Like the other wolf shifters, he was big, but the smile lines around his eyes and the broad grin on his face made him a little more approachable.

"Hi," she said awkwardly.

His smile still in place, he bowed his head. "It's a pleasure to meet you," he responded.

"And this is Tony. He's visiting from the Blue Ridge Pack in Oklahoma," Austin continued.

The other man at the table was just as big as Colt but much more serious. His eyes held so much worry in them Kiley felt a strong urge to offer him a hug. And she never wanted to do that. It surprised her, so she simply dipped her chin in respect. If she had to guess, this man had come to talk about the wolf shifters going public.

Being Rogue, she didn't have to worry about whether or not her Pack would choose to agree. Or, she *hadn't* been worried about it. A threat to Jesse was not something she would allow. She might not be a part of Tyler's Pack, but Kiley wouldn't let any of them be harmed.

"Daddy!" Jesse yelled and leapt out of Dominic's lap and across the room.

Kiley turned around to see the Alpha enter the kitchen, grinning. She found herself with her back against Austin's chest and, if she leaned *just* enough, felt a slight pressure, which Austin didn't seem to mind. Austin placed his palm at her hip and she tried to ignore the tingle.

Tyler laughed and bent to scoop Jesse up as she ran to him. "Hey, baby girl."

"Me and Kiley..."

"Kiley and I," Tyler corrected.

Jesse scrunched up her face and sighed heavily. "Kiley and I..." she repeated. "We're gonna make cookies!"

The Alpha's eyes darted to her. "I don't know if I carry

that much home insurance."

Kiley's mouth dropped open. *Oh no, he did not just say that!* She threw her arms up in the air. "One time!" she cried. "And it wasn't even my fault!"

"Kiley, you set a table on fire," Gray reminded her.

She glared at him before glancing at Austin. "It wasn't my fault."

He nodded in agreement, but his lips quirked as though he was trying to keep from laughing. She sighed and relaxed against him again, thinking of the day they were talking about.

Kiley avoided going up to the main house as much as possible. But it had been Jesse's birthday and she couldn't have missed it for any reason. Sometime while she'd been there, Gray and Dominic had put her in charge of the grill when they'd gone to get Jesse's new bike out of the house.

Then all Hell had broken loose. The flame had somehow caught on a tablecloth, which had blazed up so quickly Kiley had still been staring at it when the fire moved to the chairs. Dom had dropped his end of the bike and hurried over to put out the flames, with Gray and Tyler standing gaping at her. Luckily no one had been hurt and the food had been saved, but Kiley hadn't gotten cooking detail since. They loved to tease her about it still. She didn't mind too much—except it made her feel like family, like Pack. And she wasn't either of those things.

Kiley shivered when Austin pressed his mouth close to her ear. "I have plenty of home insurance," he promised.

She resisted rolling her eyes while he chuckled softly.

"You know, I'd buy you whatever cookies you wanted," Tyler said.

"Daddy!" Jesse's squeal came loudly. "We have to make them. That way they will be extra special."

"Of course," Tyler agreed, like he agreed to anything Jesse wanted.

"So when is this fun going to happen?" Tyler asked, glancing at her.

"As soon as I get back," Kiley answered.

"Back?" Austin and Tyler echoed at the same time.

"I need go to my apartment and pick up some clothes and my laptop. I still have a business to run," Kiley said. "It shouldn't take me longer than an hour or so if someone will watch Jesse."

"I can watch the pup," Dom offered.

"Great," Kiley said, standing. She ran her fingers lightly over Jesse's stomach, making the little girl giggle.

"That's fine with me," Tyler said. "But I don't like the idea of you leaving the property."

Kiley shrugged. "I won't be gone long."

Austin let go of her to step into her eyeline. "One of my men will accompany you."

She stiffened. Just what she'd expected. Now she would see the Alpha come out of him. "I don't think so."

"It will be safer for you to have an escort," he tried.

"An escort?" she repeated. "That's not going to happen. I'm a big girl and I can take care of myself."

"It would—"

Kiley held up her hand to cut Tyler off. She could only deal with one Alpha at a time.

"I don't know your men. I don't even know you, really. You don't get to make decisions for me," she said.

"I'm only offering you backup," Austin said.

Oh, she hated that he sounded so calm. Didn't he ever get angry? Not that she wanted to see him mad. But she wouldn't be afraid.

"I don't need backup to pack a damn bag," Kiley argued.

"It's merely a precaution. Let someone who knows what they're dealing with help," Austin pleaded. "They'll drive you to your apartment and back."

"Just a ride?" she asked.

Austin nodded before he motioned to his Beta.

"And I sit quietly like a good little pup while my chauffeur makes any stops I want?" she asked.

He flinched—at least the sarcasm was not lost on him.

"Umm...well," Austin stammered.

"So the little-bitty woman needs a strong man to act as her guard?" Kiley continued to taunt. Oh, such typical Alpha behavior.

She followed Austin's gaze as he glanced at Tyler, whose lips twitched. He wouldn't find help there, she knew. He looked over at Gray, but he had his head bent to the table. Sitting next to Gray, Tony also avoided looking at Austin. Dominic had turned away, with Jesse on his lap staring at them. Colt sat there with his eyes wide and mouth open. It seemed like the other men knew he'd messed up. Kiley pushed down amusement, since Austin obviously had no idea what to say.

"No, that's not what I meant..."

He'd narrowed his eyes, which had her angry again.

"Of course it is!" Kiley exclaimed. "Because to you, since I'm female, I'm a weaker shifter." She poked him in the chest. "Well, let me tell you something, Alpha," she continued. "I do not hide behind a man, human or shifter. I can and will take care of my damn self and if you get in my way, I'll take you down. I don't care if you're an Alpha or not."

Austin took a step back and raised his hands. "Hey now! I wasn't trying to—"

"I can't believe you!" she hissed. "Just because I let you fu—"

His hand covered her mouth so fast Kiley could only blink at him in surprise. She'd not expected that move. Austin pressed up close enough to her that he barely had to lower his head. "Stop right there," he said.

A shiver racked her body from the intimacy of the contact.

"My concern for you might stem from our past night together, but I wouldn't put my own Pack at risk for no reason. We believe the threat is real. If you leave the territory, we can't protect you and they could use you to get to us." He dropped his hand from her mouth as she continued to stare into his hard gaze.

It was hard to concentrate on what he'd said, but she managed to shove down the need coursing through her. "How?" she argued. "I'm not part of this Pack. How is anyone going to use me?"

Austin shook his head. "You might not officially be a member, but we both know your feelings for the people in this room are strong. You've bonded with them, whether you like it or not."

His words were a slap in the face. All of the anger and resentment fled and she stared at him open-mouthed. Austin was right. She might not be a registered member of the Pack, but she had connected with them. Jesse, Gray, Tyler and even Dom. They'd shared dinners together, laughed and spent time with one another. Even if she'd been fighting it and tried not to let them in, Kiley had failed. She'd begun to care deeply for them.

Austin nodded as though he knew what she was thinking.

"No." She murmured the word at him.

"It's true," he said.

Kiley pushed at him. It wasn't his fault, but she felt like punching him for pointing out that as hard as she'd tried to not form bonds with other shifters, she'd still managed to put herself in danger again. If she trusted another shifter and they treated her the way Riker had, then Kiley knew she wouldn't survive a second time.

"I don't know what happened to make you hate being in a Pack so much, but if you really think about it, I believe you'll see you've found a home without realizing it," Austin told her.

Kiley's stomach cramped. Too many emotions were bubbling to the surface and she needed time to herself. She straightened up and fisted her hands while she glared at Austin. If he thought he would be able to use this information to trap her into a relationship, he would soon learn she couldn't be controlled.

"I'm going to my apartment to get my stuff," she said, as coolly as possible. "I do not want company. I will be back in less than an hour." With those final words, she spun on her heel and marched out of the kitchen. She did not scan the room—they'd all remained silent during her and Austin's exchange.

There was little chance no one else had heard their conversation and Kiley felt beyond embarrassed. Escape— she needed an escape. Time to get her head wrapped around what Austin had made her realize, as well as figure out how to bury her feelings for him down deep.

She stomped through the house and outside until she reached her vehicle. Kiley glanced around to make sure no one else was in sight before opening the door and climbing behind the wheel. One hour—hopefully she would have regained control by then.

If not, Kiley stood in real danger of losing everything, but especially the freedom and security she'd worked so hard to have. She wouldn't explain to Austin why she was the way she was. No, instead, she needed a sure-fire plan to push him away for good.

Kiley couldn't believe how much relief she felt when she drove through the gates leading her away from the Alpha compound. She felt grateful no one tried to stop her. Her wolf raised its head, close to the surface, and no poor innocent guard deserved her anger.

The radio remained off for her to sort through her jumbled thoughts.

Until yesterday, Kiley had been happy with her existence. Or as happy as she'd been about anything. From the beginning of her new life, she'd decided she wouldn't be known as a victim. The day she'd escaped, Kiley had remade herself from a scared victim into the strong woman she was now. No way would she return to letting anyone have control of her.

That meant she'd have to distance herself from Tyler and the Pack and never see Austin again. Her heart ached at the thought, but surviving stood higher on her list of priorities.

As soon as Jesse stood clear once more of any danger,

Kiley would leave town. Start over and become someone new, where she would be able to stop herself from growing attached to anyone again.

Kiley glanced into the rear-view mirror the way she'd been doing every few minutes since she'd begun driving. She hadn't missed the tail she'd had since leaving Tyler's house. Another vehicle had pulled behind her not long after she'd exited the territory and had been following at a slower pace. She circled her block a couple of times just to make sure. Since Tyler and his men already knew where she lived, it must be either one of Austin's men or Austin had been right and she stood in danger.

She could call Tyler and ask for him to send some help, but that would only show Austin she did need someone. And Kiley was not about to let anyone know that. Even if she was being targeted, Kiley would take at least some of her attackers with her. The SUV on her tail wasn't getting close enough for her to see how many people were following, but if they knew anything about shifters, it would be more than one.

Gathering her confidence, she pulled into her underground garage and parked in her designated spot. She exited her SUV and waited, her hand behind her with her knife against her palm. She was registered to carry a firearm, but Kiley hadn't grabbed her gun that morning, since she had only planned on watching a cheating spouse.

It didn't take long for the big black sports utility vehicle to show up. Kiley waved at the driver just to be a smartass. The windows were too dark to see inside, but she smiled, anyway, as though she knew what she faced within. The SUV pulled up in front of her and the passenger window rolled down.

"Austin?" she asked, surprised.

It wasn't a real question, but he nodded anyway.

"What are you doing?"

"You know what I'm doing. I'm keeping an eye on you, like I said you needed," he stated sternly. "What would you have done if it wasn't me tracking you?"

Kiley brought her arm around, showing him her deadly weapon.

Austin shook his head. "You'd have to get pretty close to use that. And what if there'd been more than one?"

"I'm not a novice," she told him. She'd trained for a year with the best self-defense guru in the city. She still had sessions twice a week with Master Woo.

Austin merely continued to stare at her.

She blew out a breath and counted to ten—slowly. Austin didn't speak, but he sighed and she felt his gaze on her.

"Park over there," she told him, waving to the nearest visitors' spot. "You might as well come up."

He pressed his lips together and sat quietly for a moment before rolling up the window and complying. When he'd gotten out of the SUV and joined her, Kiley led the way up the stairs and into her building.

Neither spoke and Kiley's nerves were frayed. Less than five minutes ago, she had convinced herself to stay as far away from Austin as possible while distancing herself from the others. Now all she wanted to do was to cuddle into Austin's strength and let him take care of her for a while. A short while, but just enough to give her a break. She couldn't, though, and that made her tense.

Austin followed her to the elevator and she pressed the button to be taken to her floor. The ride didn't last long, but she was still relieved to get out. Being so close to Austin made her feel uneasy. Well, *uneasy* wasn't the right word. His musky scent played havoc with her hormones and she itched to touch him. Instead of giving in, she stomped down the hall and unlocked her door before she stepped aside and let him enter first.

It trembled on the tip of her tongue to ask if he wanted to check her closet for monsters. But that probably wouldn't help the situation. Instead, she watched him take in her small but clean and comfortable home.

The front door led into a spacious open-concept

apartment. The living room stood to the left, containing a black leather couch and chair, balanced to the right by the open full kitchen with its island in the middle. Straight ahead were the bedroom and bathroom doors. Her style was simple but elegant, or so she thought. She was secretly pleased when he whistled.

"Nice place," he told her.

"Thanks." She waved him forward. "Would you like a drink?"

Austin shook his head and walked over to the full-length windows behind the couch. "Pretty view of the mountains."

Kiley took her gaze from him and looked at the scene he was enjoying. *It is a wonderful view.* Tyler had helped her to get the place and she rejoiced every day that she'd agreed to take a look. She'd jumped at the chance to move in. Thinking about it now, finding her apartment had been the beginning of when she'd started trusting the Alpha.

Now she had another Alpha she either had to trust or find some other way to get rid of. Kiley knew if she told Austin exactly why she avoided Packs and more than one night with any man, he'd see her for how she really stood. A fucked-up, soiled woman who wasn't worth his time.

She hadn't told anyone other than Tyler and Gray, but now her choices were being taken away from her. As much as Kiley didn't want a confession time, what else could she do to get Austin to turn tail and run? Ten minutes, and she would be on her own again. Ten minutes of cutting her wrists and letting him watch her bleed, but Kiley needed to get it done.

"Will you sit down? We need to talk," she requested.

Austin turned and, with a look of apprehension, nodded and sat on the couch. Kiley took the chair across from him and curled her feet under her.

"First, I want to say I'm sorry about what I said in the kitchen," she told him. It would be the only time she ever told him she was sorry. Not many heard the words from her—they weren't something she made a habit of saying.

"You didn't deserve to be treated like that, especially not in front of the others. I'm sorry."

He looked surprised but nodded slowly.

"I have a tendency to go off sometimes and say things without thinking them through. I overreacted," she added. She pressed on, just letting the words flow.

"Kiley...I..." Austin started. He leaned forward, resting his elbows on his knees, and dropped his head. "I understand you have a problem with my position. I don't know why, but I can see it bothers you. Please tell me what's going on."

Oh, where to start? "You know I'm Rogue?" she asked.

"Tyler told me that much," he responded gently. The compassion in his eyes showed her that while he might not have all the details, he was aware her past held pain.

"I left the Pack after Tyler took over. I didn't have the choice to do it with the previous leader. My father had demanded I marry the Alpha," she explained. "I couldn't stand the man. He was loud and abusive and made my skin crawl."

"Your father didn't know?" he asked.

"Oh, he knew," she assured him. "He just didn't care."

"But why would he..."

Kiley shook her head. "I didn't grow up with a father like Jesse's. Instead of letting me go when I begged, he gave me over to the Alpha when I turned eighteen. He didn't care about me, just what Riker would give him for me."

"Fuck, *Riker*," Austin spat.

"Yeah," Kiley agreed. She knew Austin would piece things together when he heard Riker's name. "It wasn't good. I won't go into detail now, but it was bad for a really long time. I had no choice in anything I did. I had to follow orders, and that was that."

"I'm sorry." He scooted off the couch and knelt in front of her.

"What are you sorry for?" she asked, confused.

"It upsets you to talk about this."

"It does," she confirmed. "I don't have great memories

from my childhood, but as an adult, it was even worse. For the first time in my life, I'm on my own. I feel I finally have control of my life."

"And here I come along, confusing things."

"Exactly," Kiley said. "The night we spent together was perfect, but it has to be only one night."

"What if that night was just the beginning for us? It might be your chance at a much better life."

"I did that on my own. I don't need a man to make my life better," Kiley told him.

Kiley squealed in surprise when Austin grabbed her and planted her in his lap. "You don't listen to me."

She didn't mind the position she found herself in, but the disappointment in his voice bothered her. "What?"

He cupped her face, gently making her look him in the eye. "I said that night might be your chance at a better life. I know you've picked yourself up off the ground and are strong. Hell, I can feel the power inside you. You're one of the strongest females I've ever met. If you put your mind to it, you could probably become an Alpha."

Kiley scoffed. "Like I'd ever want that."

"No, you wouldn't," Austin agreed. "But you *could*. That's what I'm saying."

"What does this have to do with anything?" Kiley snapped. As much as she enjoyed feeling him under her, Kiley didn't like the direction this conversation was headed toward. She was ready to confess what had happened to her, but Austin wasn't letting her push him away.

"It means you've proven you can survive and have power. The thing is, you're still letting Riker have control over you."

"I am not!"

Austin stroked her cheek. "You're pushing me away, all of us, because you don't want to trust anyone. Riker's abuse is still right here." He tapped her temple. "And by not opening yourself up and taking a chance, he wins."

Kiley pushed at his chest to try to get away, but Austin

slid his free arm around her waist.

"Don't," he said. "You're going to have to let someone love you. Why not me?"

Kiley laughed uneasily. "What? *Love* me?"

"Maybe," he said. "One day. But if you don't give me the chance, how will we know?"

"You may be building yourself up for a big fall. You don't even know me."

"No, no, I'm not. And, yes, I do. I know what I see when I look into your eyes. I am connected with you, even after one night," he told her, then kissed her.

The kiss was soft, a mere meeting of lips. Kiley relaxed into the first intimate touch from him. Austin ran his tongue over her bottom lip before he nibbled the soft flesh. She opened with a gasp and he slid his tongue inside. Her whole body came alive instantly. His taste, spicy and manly, burst in her mouth and she moaned, wrapping her arms around his neck. She smelled his arousal and it made her body ache with need.

Her panties were catching the liquid escaping from her sex and she shifted in his arms, trying to relieve the pressure. He broke the kiss and rested his forehead against hers.

"God, Kiley."

He didn't need to say any more. She knew exactly what he meant. "Yes, Austin, kiss me again," she urged.

He growled and slammed his mouth down on hers. This time the heat came quickly. Her head swam with the passion she felt for him until she found herself straddling his lap, humping him.

"Hot...need," she panted out against his lips. The rutting instinct was strong and she didn't want to fight it. She was so tired of fighting. In Austin's arms, she could let go.

"Yeah," he agreed, his voice low and husky. He stood, picking her up with him. She wrapped her legs around his waist. "Bedroom?"

"First door," she told him before sealing her mouth on his neck.

She sucked and nibbled the muscled flesh, running her tongue over him and tasting. His jugular pulsed as she paid special attention to that spot, biting down gently but not breaking the skin. He stumbled and tightened his arms around her.

"Don't stop," he ordered, his breath coming in short bursts.

Kiley was more than happy to listen to that demand. He made it to the bedroom door and threw it open while she gave him little love bites up and down his neck.

"Good, your mouth is so good," he told her.

"Mmm hmm," she murmured.

They didn't turn on any lights. Austin clumsily made his way to the bed. He fell on it with her underneath him. Kiley pulled his shirt over his head to run her palms over his strong, wide shoulders.

"I've wanted to touch your bare skin since I saw you again."

Austin looked up from where he was pulling off her boots and socks. "I know…I know…"

They undressed each other quickly but still took the time to explore each new inch of flesh revealed. By the time he covered her body with his once again, Kiley trembled. She wrapped her legs high up on his back, feeling his hard, ready cock at her pussy.

"Please, I need to feel you inside me," she told him breathlessly. Her entire body was flushed and she knew once he was inside her, it wouldn't take long for them to reach climax. The connection was simply so strong and only having him fill her was going to take care of the ache between her legs.

He groaned long and loud, saturating the quiet room with the sound. He pushed in slowly, but Kiley didn't want him to be gentle. She dropped her feet onto the mattress and bucked her hips, taking him in deep. They moaned in unison.

"Fuck!" he exclaimed. "So tight. Hot and tight." Austin

peppered her collarbone with small kisses and nips.

Kiley dug her fingernails into his shoulders. "Move, hurry."

He pulled out, plunging in once more.

"Yes! Yes!" she cried out. He filled her completely. More than just her body. With him thrusting in and out, she felt their souls connect. She almost panicked, but Austin placed his mouth over hers and her fear left.

Austin snapped his hips while Kiley continued to meet each thrust. He ripped his mouth from hers, grunting.

"Austin!" she cried in pleasure.

"God... Oh, God..." he chanted. He pistoned faster and faster.

Kiley barely heard his words. She thrashed her head back and forth on the pillow and arched to meet every stroke. Her body shook and, like an explosion, she came apart.

Dimly, she heard herself scream. Austin's voice was hoarse while he rocked into her. She clamped her inner muscles down on his cock and he yelled before he came. His hot seed flooded her pussy and she wrapped her arms around his neck to hold him tight.

Maybe they would have this second night together. It was all she'd really ask for. Austin had been right about so much. If she didn't start opening herself up to others, she'd let Riker win. Kiley closed her eyes while Austin nuzzled her neck.

She wasn't ready for Pack, though, and the man in bed with her was an Alpha. So, no matter how far she'd gotten from Riker's abuse, there was still something she couldn't have. Him, for longer than a night.

"Stop thinking," Austin murmured. "We don't have much more time. We have to get to Tyler's and I want to enjoy this sated feeling. I can't if you're all tense."

Kiley laughed. "So sorry."

He grunted at her and Kiley patted his back. He was right. There'd be plenty of time for her to worry later.

Chapter Three

"Drive with me," Austin asked softly while carrying Kiley's bags for her into the parking garage. He didn't want her to feel he was demanding it — he only wanted her close. He had a feeling that as soon as Kiley was alone, she'd start thinking anything between the two of them wouldn't work. He needed a chance to convince her differently, but time wasn't on his side.

She stopped walking but didn't pull away, which was an improvement.

"I can't," she whispered. "Please understand, Austin. I can't be without a way to leave. I'm not saying I will leave again, but I have to have a way."

He held her cheek. Their eyes locked and Austin saw the emotions there, saw how important this one thing was to her. It had more to do with Riker's influence on her life than anything else. Fuck, he wished he'd been the one to find Riker. Instead of the old Alpha being delivered to the Council, Austin would have ended his existence. Now it was too late. Riker would never see the light of day again, but that also meant Austin couldn't get his hands on him. All he could do was try to repair the damage Riker had inflicted on Kiley and those in his Pack.

"Okay, no problem." He'd give her what she needed.

Her relief was so noticeable she actually shook with it.

"Thank you," she told him with a smile and pushed up against him.

Austin bent his head, unable to resist her luscious lips, and sealed his mouth over hers. Kiley responded quickly, wrapping her arms around his neck and opening to him.

He held in a groan as he pulled her body flush with his. It felt so wonderful to hold her. The sudden squeal of tires broke the moment and he pulled away in time to see a big, dark SUV racing toward them.

Instincts kicked in. He threw her bags between two cars, pushed her after them and jumped to cover her body with his.

Metal scraped metal when the SUV hit one of the parked cars. Kiley screamed and his wolf howled inside at her fear. Austin leapt to his feet as the SUV reversed. He couldn't see inside the dark interior, but he'd smelled shifter. He grabbed hold of Kiley's arms and yanked her up.

"Go around the front and get into your car!" he ordered.

Without hesitation, she scrambled to comply. She grabbed the bags at her feet and darted in front of the car that had shielded them. Austin stepped out into the parking lot the second the SUV lurched forward, as if taunting him.

Austin smiled grimly. He'd always been a pretty easygoing guy, but threaten an innocent, and he felt like feeding someone their own balls. After he'd ripped them off. He narrowed his eyes and waited. The vehicle sat only about fifteen yards from him. Whoever was inside would clearly see his challenge. From the corner of his eye, he glimpsed movement and knew it was Kiley. He couldn't look at her, but as soon as they were safe, he'd give her a piece of his mind.

The attacker gunned the engine of the vehicle again.

Kiley moved farther into view and he saw her aiming a gun at the back passenger window.

"Kiley." He growled her name. They needed whoever was inside alive so they had a chance to get information out of them.

He didn't get time to come up with a plan, though. The SUV sped in reverse and was out of sight in seconds. His first instinct was to follow, but he needed to make sure Kiley was unharmed first.

He hurried over to her and grabbed her wrist. "Where did

you get that?"

"My apartment," she said.

She stared after the SUV and, by the way she rocked on the balls of her feet, Kiley wanted to follow. No way was he allowing that.

"Stay," he ordered and tightened his grip just to make sure she complied. He punched the first Speed Dial with his thumb. As soon as Colt answered, Austin barked out orders. "Get to Kiley's apartment ASAP! Bring plenty of help. Leave Tyler at the house and make sure Jesse is guarded."

Colt's calm voice assured Austin he was already on his way and everything would be handled. He didn't ask any questions and Austin was glad. He needed his Beta by his side. Colt would be able to keep him calm so he didn't totally screw up things with Kiley. Even then, with his blood pumping hard, fueled by adrenaline, he recognized the Alpha wolf wanting to take over. Kiley stared at the hand he had wrapped around her wrist and he loosened his hold but didn't let go of her completely.

He needed to get himself together before the others arrived. He still had the scent of the shifter who had come after them. Austin hadn't been able to see behind the blackened window, but his nose had told him all he'd needed to know. The scent of the ones who would now become the prey for putting Kiley at risk, just when he was getting his chance to be with her.

Austin shoved his phone into his pocket after Colt had disconnected.

"Are you okay?" he asked, running his gaze over her to make sure she hadn't sustained any injuries when he'd pushed her to the ground.

"Yes, you?" She looked at him with wide eyes.

"The adrenaline is waning," he noted. Kiley tilted to the side and he reached out to steady her.

She nodded. "Think so."

"It's okay," he murmured, pulling her close. "I've got

you." Austin led Kiley to the driver's side of her vehicle for her to sit and catch her breath.

Kiley had been brave and, even though he wished she'd let him handle the attack, he was proud she'd stood up for herself. The unknown shifters could have been after either of them and he hated not knowing what was going on.

"Just relax," he said, opening the door and gently helping her inside. Austin took her face between his hands and kissed her softly on her lips.

Her eyes were cloudy with confusion. "You're not hurt, right?" she asked.

"I'm not hurt," he assured her. "Help is on the way and then we'll get back to the Alpha house."

She nodded, absently rubbing at her right knee. Austin carefully pushed her hand away and saw a rip in her jeans. He smelled the blood under the material, along with dirt and grit.

Austin ground his teeth to hold in the wolf. She had been hurt.

"I need to check on Jesse," she said quietly.

"Okay," he agreed. "You do that. I'm going to see if I can pick up any more scents."

Kiley pulled out her cell and Austin walked away to give her privacy and to do what he'd said he would. Find the shifters who had attacked.

Kiley watched from the front of her SUV while Austin ordered his men around, making sure they got everything they needed from the scene. He'd been pissed when Tyler had shown up with Colt and Dominic. Kiley saw it in the way he'd glared at the other Alpha while he watched his men. She would have been amused by the obvious over-protectiveness if she hadn't been so shaken up.

Even when they'd asked her to guard Jesse, she hadn't taken the threat seriously. Who'd attack two Alphas surrounded by Pack? Kiley'd thought she'd be a glorified babysitter while the Alphas held the meetings. Now she knew differently. Someone, shifters, had tried to run them down. She was anxious to return to the house and see Jesse to make sure the young girl was indeed safe.

If she concentrated on keeping Jesse unharmed, that would also give her time to think on what she was going to do about Austin. All her plans and ideas had flown out of the window when he'd been in danger. All she'd been able to could think was that she had to protect him. Austin had thought she'd been shaking because of adrenaline, but the truth was she'd been scared for him.

"Shit," she muttered. How had everything gotten so messed up? Kiley was barely getting her head wrapped around realizing she'd bonded with Tyler and the others. Now she had real strong feeling for an Alpha shifter. Hell, she was halfway in love with him and she didn't even know him.

Austin walked over to her and she had to look away since her emotions were so close to the surface. He'd put himself in danger to protect her. No one had ever done that for her. It had brought up too many feelings for her to be able to easily separate and process. Feelings she had spent a long time trying to bury.

Austin stroked her cheek and lifted her face with a soft finger to place an even softer kiss on her lips. The tender gesture was too much and she had to pull away and drop her chin to hide the tears that wanted to fall. He was so damn sweet.

"Gray and Tony are on their way. They were across town when we called. The minute they get here, we'll head to Tyler's."

Kiley started to relax against him as he gently rubbed circles on the small of her back. "Okay," she managed to whisper.

She allowed him to hold her until Tyler walked over. Then her instinct to show no weakness in front of others kicked in and she pulled away. Austin let go of her with a heavy sigh. Luckily, Tyler forestalled anything Austin would have said.

"How are you doing, kid?" Tyler asked.

Kiley rolled her eyes but laughed, which was no doubt the reaction he wanted. He gave everyone stupid little nicknames. The first time he'd called her kid, she had reminded him he was only about three years older than her.

He'd responded that it didn't matter because when Kiley hung out with Jesse, it was as though she was a kid herself again. She'd thought long and hard about that and had eventually agreed. When she was with Jesse, she did feel ten, fifteen years younger, getting to do all the things she had never done while a child. She enjoyed playing games, swimming and spending time with the little cub. It had even made her think about having her own kids one day. She had been almost certain she wouldn't, but now the possibility was there. She wondered if Austin wanted children.

She didn't realize she'd gone off into her own thoughts until Austin pressed harder on her back and she glanced up to see matching looks of concern on his and Tyler's faces.

"Sorry," she mumbled. "I'm fine. Really."

Tyler nodded while Austin stared at her as though he wasn't buying it.

"I promise, Austin. I was thinking…"

"You'd tell me…" he asked, dropping his voice low so only she heard. "You'd tell me if you weren't okay?"

"Yes," she assured him.

He took a deep breath and she watched the play of his muscles over his stomach. A stomach she wanted to spend hours licking and tasting. She wanted to have him all around her. Surrounding her, filling her, consuming her. She felt flushed, hot and needy. She smelled him — rich, sweet and woodsy.

Austin chuckled and she gasped, caught once again lost in her own thoughts. Except this time, she'd been busted fantasizing about Austin. But when he turned his body into hers, discreetly rubbing his erection against her thigh, she knew she wasn't the only one longing to reconnect in the way they had earlier.

"Austin." She whispered his name with need.

Tyler's phone rang and he stepped away, which relieved her.

"I want you," Austin told her, sliding his hands up her thighs.

She wanted to squirm and beg. That was a new feeling and she didn't know what to do about it. Her instincts told her to grab hold of Austin and pull him in close. Kiley clutched the nape of his neck and tugged until their mouths were only a breath apart. She closed her eyes, taking his mouth with hers.

Kiley growled when their lips pressed together, nipping to demand entrance. He opened for her and she swept her tongue inside, tasting him. Spicy and strong, Austin was the best-tasting man she'd ever had the pleasure of savoring. Kiley was leaning into him when Tyler's curse broke through the fog in her mind.

"What's wrong?" Austin spun around to face Tyler while blocking her from any threat that might be near.

"Tony was shot," Tyler told them, still holding the phone up to his ear.

She gasped, unable to hold it in, even as she brought up her hands to grip the back of Austin's shirt.

"Yes, Gray," Tyler said into his cell. "We'll be right there."

Tyler disconnected the call before facing them. "They were on the way here when a black SUV pulled up beside them and opened fire. Tony was in the passenger seat and was hit."

"Let's go."

Austin motioned for Kiley to climb over to the other seat then followed her and got behind the wheel. Tyler already had the back door opened and had jumped inside.

Kiley put her hand on her stomach when Austin sped out of the parking space to race her vehicle from the garage. Someone she knew had been shot and Kiley shook with fear.

In all honesty, she had been concerned about the threats but hadn't really thought the Pack were in real danger. Even earlier in the garage had seemed more of a warning than someone trying to kill them. No one spoke as they sped down the streets to where Gray and Tony were supposed to be. Austin took a sharp right and spotted a police car with its lights flashing behind Gray's vehicle. Austin slammed his foot on the brakes and they slid to a stop, almost ramming the cop car.

Tyler and Austin were out of her SUV so fast they were mere blurs. Kiley was still trying to get her door open when she saw Tyler grasping Gray and yanking him close and Austin bending down and peering into the open passenger door. Kiley climbed slowly out of her vehicle and slammed the door behind her. The cop glanced at her and she recognized him—he was a member of Tyler's Pack. That was good. At least they wouldn't have to worry about human interference. This would need to be handled by the Pack.

As she walked closer, Austin motioned her forward. She hurried to his side and saw Tony sitting grinning at them.

"I was shot in the arm," Tony told her. "It barely even hurts."

Since he was pale and shaking, Kiley didn't believe him. "Sure," she responded. "Why don't you get out of the car and we'll dance right here on the side of the road. You can rumba, right?"

Austin snorted while Tony glared at her.

"Smartass," Tony mumbled. "I hoped you'd be on my side."

"I am," she said, crouching down. "Someone tried to kill you, though."

"I don't think so," Tony said.

Kiley felt movement behind her and swung around to see Tyler and Gray had joined them. She shifted enough so neither man was at her back.

"What do you mean?" Austin asked.

"They were shooting at the vehicle, but they could have driven right up and aimed in through my window. Instead, they took pot shots at the car and I got hit by accident," Tony said.

"What do you think?" Austin asked Gray.

Gray shrugged.

"Oh, come on!" Tony leaned over then winced.

"Okay," Gray said. "I agree with Tony. But the fact is you *were* shot."

Tony sighed. "Cain's going to be pissed."

Both Austin and Tyler chuckled, but the sound had a nervous tinge to it.

"Alpha." The cop strolled over. "We're garnering a lot of attention. We need to move this along. Another police car might roll in to check out the scene at any time."

"Gray, get Tony back to the house. We'll treat his wound there," Tyler said. "Austin and Kiley, I need you both to follow behind them and make sure they get there safely."

"What are you going to do?" Austin asked.

"Shift and see if I can pick up a scent. They would have left someone close by to watch what we do. I'm going to try to find them first," Tyler stated.

"Not by yourself," Gray argued.

Tyler simply lifted an eyebrow. "I do believe I'm the Alpha here."

"Not the only Alpha," Austin growled. "I'll stay. You take care of your Pack."

"This is my responsibility," Tyler said.

"And you're my friend." Austin squeezed Kiley's shoulder before he stood and faced Tyler. "Let me do this for you. I'll make my report and once we have the Pack settled, we'll figure out what to do."

Kiley rose, too. She didn't want Austin out on his own any more than she wanted Tyler. "I can help."

"No." Austin whirled on her. "You need to get to the house and look after Jesse. If they are trying to scare us or give us warnings, they might try to take Jesse to get Tyler to do whatever they want. She's in the greatest danger."

"Shit!" Kiley spun around and raced to her car. Austin was right—taking Jesse would ensure Tyler would do anything to get her back safely. Jesse was the Alpha's entire world.

By the time she was behind the wheel and had the car started, Tyler yanked open the other door.

"Come on," she yelled at him.

"Dom's got Jesse," Tyler told her. "Calm down and follow behind Gray. We have to make sure we all get there safely."

Kiley glanced through the windshield at Austin. "What about him?"

"Austin will be okay," Tyler said, patting her hand. "He's a strong wolf and he wants to help. He'll protect all of us. Especially you."

Kiley really didn't want to get into a conversation about the relationship, or whatever the hell was going on, between her and Austin. "If he gets hurt—"

"He won't," Tyler said. "I texted Colt, Austin's Beta, and he's headed over here to help Austin then bring him back to us."

Kiley sighed. Gray flashed his brake lights at her before he pulled off the side and onto the street. Austin raised his hand to her and she nodded at him. She'd see him at the house. A few hours, and they would both be behind the gates and the protection of the wolves. It would be okay.

She followed behind Gray, making sure to keep her gaze all around them in case there were any other problems. The entire drive into Pack territory was tense and silent. Tyler was also searching for trouble, keeping an eye out. When they passed through the gates, Kiley tried to relax. Her shoulders ached from driving with her hands tight on the steering column and from sitting stiffly.

"We're home." The relief in Tyler's voice was evident.

"How many guards are on duty?" she asked.

"All of them," Tyler said.

"Okay. I won't let Jesse out of my sight."

"I know. It's why I asked Gray to bring you to us."

Pride and comfort filled her. Kiley stopped her car in front of the Alpha house and gazed up at the monstrous building. "I'm glad you're building a new house," she whispered.

"Me, too," he said quietly. "I want to raise Jesse in a house full of love and laughter. We're never going to have that inside here."

"No," Kiley said. "Not here."

"I had hoped that if we built a new home, you would come around more. I know Jesse misses you."

"Hoped?" she asked, turning toward him.

Tyler smiled and grasped her hand. "I think something bigger is in store for you."

She shook her head. "You're talking about Austin."

"Of course I'm talking about Austin."

"I don't know what's happening between us. Or what can happen. He doesn't even live here," she said.

"And you've never found a home here," he pointed out.

"I have a home," she argued.

"No. You hide out in the shadows."

His words hurt her a little. Kiley dropped her gaze to her lap. "I've gotten better."

"You have. But what if you didn't have to stay here? What if where you're needed is with others who have been through Riker's terror?"

"Austin's Pack," she said.

"Yes. There are others who fled there because they couldn't remain in this territory. He's a strong Alpha who will protect them and make sure they are never harmed again."

"So, what I can do?" she asked.

"You can be the buffer between Packs," Tyler said. "Austin's original Pack is trying to welcome the ones from Riker's, but your old Pack is having trouble trusting them. You can help them."

"I can't be a part of his Pack," she told him. "Any Pack."

Tyler shook his head. "I don't believe that. I think when you find the right fit, you'll be perfect. In the meantime, you don't have to be a member of Austin's Pack to help them."

"They don't even know who I am," she pointed out. Riker had made damn sure no one other than his most faithful had had any clue that Kiley had been held hostage in the compound.

"They know of you," Tyler said. "Your treatment was one of the most serious crimes Riker was convicted of."

She shuddered. Kiley had never wanted anyone to know what had happened to her. She'd never even told Tyler everything she'd gone through. When the Alpha Council had questioned her, they'd promised Kiley that no-one else would know the details.

"Things about the trial slipped out," Tyler said. "The Council did their best to keep things real quiet, but a lot of people were involved."

The sense of betrayal that coursed through her was surprising. She hadn't really known what to believe when she'd met with the Council but had hoped that they'd be able to keep Riker locked up for the rest of her life. In the assurances they'd given her, Kiley knew there was still a chance her story would get out. She'd taken the opportunity knowing that that was possible.

"It's about starting over," Tyler told her.

"What about Jesse?" she asked.

"She'll understand. Plus, Austin is one of my best friends. We see each other often."

Kiley didn't know what to say. It was true she hadn't really been living, but was leaving the best option? Damn, there was too much going on. "I need time to think."

"I'll see what I can do to help."

The front door opened and Dom stepped out.

"We should get inside," Kiley said.

"Promise me you'll think about it."

Kiley nodded. She was sure she'd think of nothing else.

Austin paced the bedroom he'd been given, thinking about everything that had happened in the last twenty-four hours. He'd found Kiley again after having pretty much given up hope that he'd ever see her again. He was thirty-six years old and he had met the woman who he was supposed to spend the rest of his life with. Austin was sure of it—Kiley belonged to him.

He was exhausted. It had been a long day and he was just starting to finally process events. Tyler had been right in thinking that whoever was behind the attacks had left someone behind to watch them. Austin had tracked the feline shifter six blocks until Colt had joined him. After he'd had help, they'd stepped up the hunt to capture the feline.

In the way of the wolves, when they worked together as a Pack, they were able to take on any other shifter. The feline had been one of the large cat species, but Austin had had no doubt they'd take him down. Austin hadn't counted on the feline having backup. Just as they had been closing in, a large black truck had shown up and the feline had leapt into the rear.

He'd gotten away, but Austin had picked up the scent.

Luckily, Tony would recover. The Pack doctor had looked him over, telling them that the bullet had gone through and Tony was going to fine. Doc Jensen had bandaged Tony up and given him some pain meds. Already, Tony's brother and some members of his Pack were on the way. Not that Austin was surprised. Tony's family was very close.

There was nothing else Austin could do at that moment. Not until Tony's Pack arrived and they decided the next step. That was why Austin paced his room.

Tyler had recalled all his members into Pack territory to stay there for their own safety. Austin agreed with him and would have made the same decision in his place. The compound could be protected more easily. He'd made a call home and warned his own Pack to be on the lookout for anything strange. He needed to see to them himself, but he didn't want to leave yet. His best friend was still in danger and he had the added complication of Kiley. Her life was here and even if she didn't belong to Tyler's Pack, she wouldn't simply leave.

Austin didn't know what to do about her. He wished he was able to go to her right then, but after dinner she'd said she'd needed to be alone and was tired. Austin didn't want to push her, but he had whispered that he'd leave his door unlocked just in case. With the hours that had passed, she'd obviously decided against spending time with him.

Resigning himself to a night alone, he stripped off his clothes before climbing into bed. The cool sheets felt good against his skin. He switched off the lamp and settled against his pillows. He'd grown painfully hard from thinking about Kiley and he lazily stroked himself. He was getting into it, pumping his hips and tightening the hand he had curled around his sex, when there was a soft knock on his door.

He sensed Kiley in the hallway and it almost sent him over the edge. He held back, barely. Austin had started to lift himself from the bed when his door opened.

"Austin?" Kiley asked in a quiet voice.

He was thrilled. Kiley had come to him. It didn't matter what she wanted or needed. If she only wanted to talk, that would be fine with him. Oh, he would like to do a whole lot more, but he would take anything he could get with her right now.

"Come in, Kiley," he encouraged.

She stepped into the room and closed the door behind her. He had no problem seeing her in the dark. She stood next to the door, dressed in pajama bottoms and a tank top, hair still wet from her shower, wringing her hands together.

He reached over to turn on the lamp.

"No," she said quickly.

He froze with his hand still in the air.

"Can I…? You said…"

Austin waited, trying to give her time to get out what she wanted to say. He hoped she wanted to spend the night in his bed after all.

She cleared her throat. "Tyler came and got Jesse. Said he wanted to put her in his bed so he could sleep. You know, having her close and all, so he'll sleep better."

Austin knew exactly what she meant. That was why he wanted Kiley.

"So, I thought, since Jesse's with him, I'd come in here. That is, if you still want me to."

Austin pressed his lips together to stop his wide grin from showing. Instead, he lifted the edge of the sheet and invited her to join him. She didn't waste any time climbing into bed with him and cuddling into his arms. Her head resting under his chin, he held her tight against his body. He'd fallen asleep with her in this way another time and when he'd opened his eyes, she'd been gone.

As hard as it was to push those memories aside, he had to. Austin understood some of what she'd been through. He needed to be patient. Needed to give her time to come to terms with her feelings. He closed his eyes, content to have her in his bed. "Thank you for coming to me," he whispered.

Her soft lips brushed against his collarbone. "I didn't want to sleep alone," she confessed softly. "Plus, I remembered how good your arms around me felt that night. It's what scared me into leaving."

"I know, but you never have to sleep alone again unless you want to," he responded. And it was the truth. He'd give her time, but that didn't mean he'd give up on her.

She sighed and her body slowly went limp against him. He lay there for a long time listening to her soft, steady breathing, happy despite everything else going on. Finally, when he was sure she wouldn't disappear on him again, he closed his eyes.

Chapter Four

Kiley woke up alone in the big bed. Not something she was happy about. Maybe Austin had wanted to give her a taste of her own medicine or some shit like that? She frowned. She didn't think he'd be that petty, but she did have trust issues. Austin had never played games, though. From the word go, he'd been brutally honest about what he wanted. And that was her. It was Kiley who kept going back and forth in her feelings. With a sigh, she climbed off the bed and quickly dressed. Before heading to find Austin, she peeked into Jesse's room. The little girl wasn't there.

Standing in the hall, she used her senses to pick up where the two people she wanted were. They were both in the kitchen. She smelled eggs, bacon, sausage, ham and coffee. Low voices were speaking, but she couldn't make out what they were saying. Knowing she would find not only Jesse but Austin, too, she headed for the kitchen. Once at the door, there came a soft bark. Tyler didn't have a dog.

She entered slowly. The kitchen was full. Gray stood at the stove, managing three large skillets. Jesse was on the floor with a man Kiley didn't know while a brown puppy sat in her lap, licking her chin. Both Jesse and the man were laughing. Austin, Tyler, Colt and an older man sat at the kitchen table.

"Kiley!" Jesse exclaimed. "Look what Cain brought me!"

Kiley looked over at the puppy Jesse held up. It was cute. A small fur ball with huge paws and big floppy ears.

"She's a Lab. I'm gonna call her Daisy," Jesse told her.

Kiley knelt in front of the girl and her new puppy. Daisy wiggled around until Jesse released her. The puppy waddled over to Kiley and jumped up and down, trying to get onto her lap. Kiley picked the little thing up, surprised by her weight.

"Wow, what a big girl," she said playfully.

Cain laughed. "That's only the beginning. She should get to be about seventy pounds."

Kiley's mouth dropped open. "Seventy?"

The man nodded with a wide grin on his face. "Yeah."

"Oh, my!" But the puppy was adorable and she saw why Jesse already loved her. Kiley cuddled it up to her face. "Hello, Daisy."

"She's my very own dog!" Jesse commented.

Kiley looked over at the table to see Tyler's reaction to that bit of news. The Alpha's attention was taken up by the stranger at the table, but Austin caught her eye and winked. She looked quickly away, embarrassed. She'd gone looking for him this morning when she really should have been thinking about how she'd handle the connection between them. Kiley was still thinking about what Tyler had said. But in reality, she didn't even know if Austin would want her to go home with him. She couldn't think about it, though, in a room full of people. Instead, she turned her attention once more to Jesse and the pup.

"This is a very good dog. It's going to take lots of hard work to take care of her, but I know you can do it," Kiley told her.

The little girl beamed.

Kiley was thrilled to see her happy. Peeking up from under her lashes, she looked at the other man on the floor. She smelled the man's mate on him and relaxed a little. He wouldn't be interested in her if he'd claimed someone as his own.

"I'm Tony's brother, Cain," he told her with a dip of his head when he saw her glancing in his direction.

"Kiley," she responded. She was glad he didn't try to take her hand or touch her.

"I know. Austin hasn't been able to take his eyes off you

since you walked in. My father asked him three times if he was okay," Cain said laughing.

Kiley blushed. She felt Austin's gaze on her. That didn't exactly tell her how Cain had heard about her. "Uh."

"I spoke to Tony last night and he said Austin was falling all over himself because of a beautiful woman," Cain said.

She glanced at Austin, who had a faint flush on his cheeks. Hot shit, was he embarrassed?

"Shut up, Cain," Austin mumbled.

Cain wasn't the only one in the room who laughed.

She placed the puppy in Jesse's arms and stood.

The older man looked up and smiled. "You must be Kiley. It is a pleasure to meet you."

Kiley blinked at him for several seconds. This man was the most powerful shifter who she'd ever been in front of, even more dominant than Austin and Tyler. She actually felt she should be bowing to him or something.

"Thank you, sir," she replied respectfully.

"I'm Lamont, Tony's father. The overgrown child on the floor also belongs to me."

She liked this man already. Kiley wasn't afraid of him, which shocked her. Since he had such a presence, she should have been cowering in the corner. "I, uh...I'm sorry Tony was hurt. I hope he gets better soon." She didn't know what else to say.

Lamont smiled and his face transformed, making him look twenty years younger. "He is already feeling much better. We'll be taking him home tomorrow, where he can recuperate fully."

Kiley was relieved to hear Tony's recovery was going well. He seemed like a really good guy, even if she hadn't had the time to know him better.

Tyler asked Lamont something, but Kiley was distracted by Austin teasing his fingers over her side. She peered down at him and had to stop herself from touching him in turn. He was so fucking handsome.

"You okay?" he whispered.

"Yeah." She glanced over at Lamont and still there was no fear. "I think so."

"Good." He tugged her until she leaned against him.

Kiley allowed herself to rest against Austin, but the second she touched him, heat seemed to bloom between them. He smiled widely before tipping back his head. She knew what he wanted, but if she bent down and kissed him, then everyone in the room would see. She wouldn't be able to hide her feelings for him from the others.

She glanced around the room to see who was paying attention, but he caught her chin in his hand.

"No," he murmured. "Just look at me."

"Okay," she said quietly.

"It doesn't have to mean more than the fact we find each other attractive," he said.

"But it does mean more than that." It was scary to admit, but Kiley had to take a chance. The people in the room were all from different Packs. Each person had a dominant side, but they were also working together. Lamont was the most powerful shifter in the room, but it was Tyler who was laying out a plan of attack. She had to let go of the pain of the past or she wasn't going to have a future. Tyler was right. She might not be ready to pack up all her shit and follow Austin, but she wasn't a coward. It was time to stop acting like one.

Austin stood, brushing her back. "If you'll excuse us for a few minutes."

No one said anything as Austin practically dragged her from the room. He pulled her behind him and up to his room.

Once inside, he slammed the door closed and pushed her against it. "Did you mean it?"

His eyes were burning with so much desire it practically made her body burn. She wanted to touch him, so she placed her palms against the soft cotton covering his chest.

"I know there is more going on this simple attraction," she admitted. "If not, I wouldn't have been thinking about you after our first time together."

"You've been so hesitant," he said.

"I know. I still am. But I can admit strong feelings have developed."

"That's all I needed to hear."

He kissed her and Kiley wrapped her arms around his neck to hold him close. She was grateful he didn't push her for more. Kiley didn't know how much more she could give. She needed this to be enough for him.

"Need to taste you," he said huskily. "All of you."

Austin flattened his body against Kiley's, nibbling his way down her neck. He was hard under his jeans and he rubbed against her softer body, adding just the right amount of friction. It felt wonderful. She trembled under him when he ran his hands up her hips and under her shirt.

She arched her back, pressing closer for him to cup her breasts. "Want you," she said.

"Yes." He yanked her shirt over her head and quickly unhooked her bra, letting the garment fall to the floor as he took one pert nipple into his mouth. He teased the tip with his tongue before sealing his lips over the little nub and sucking.

She bucked against him. "Austin!" she cried his name, clawing at him.

He didn't answer, only continued to taste her. He ran his tongue down her stomach, then dropping to his knees and pulling at the cotton pants she wore. They slid down her legs, catching and taking her panties along with them.

When she was completely nude in front of him, he pushed her hips against the door and held her there while he lowered his mouth and swiped at her inner flesh with his tongue.

"Austin!" she called out again.

"Mine," he stated hungrily and continued. He played with her, running his tongue up and down her folds and sucking on her clit until she lifted her hips, trying to get more. She spread her legs wider and he helped by placing one leg over his shoulder.

He took his time, drawing small, animalistic sounds from her. He added a finger alongside his tongue, opening her cunt and lavishing her sex.

"Please…more…more," she panted.

He added a second digit, thrusting his fingers in faster, then covered her clit, nibbling softly.

She screamed when her orgasm ripped through her body. He held her head in place as she ground herself against his mouth. Kiley fell against the wall and Austin pulled her down, urging her to lie on her back. With the fingers of one hand still buried inside her pussy, he unsnapped the button of his jeans, releasing his already leaking, straining erection.

He'd only gotten his jeans over his hips and to his knees before he replaced his fingers with his cock. He plunged inside, holding her legs open wide to the invasion.

He rode her hard and Kiley loved it.

"Yes! Yes!" she urged.

He slammed inside her over and over, each thrust a little faster and harder. There was no rhythm, simply an intense mating between the two of them. Kiley dug her nails into his shoulders and lifted her hips to accept each stroke, chanting his name.

Kiley threw back her head and yelled, coming once again, tightening around him and wanting to pull him over the edge with her.

He snapped his hips forward, his neck straining, the veins sticking out. "Perfect, so perfect."

Austin was the perfect one. The way he showed her kindness and comfort, never pushing her, and being so wonderful to all those around him. Anyone would be lucky to have him, but it was her who he was buried inside. Kiley ran her hands up his sweaty back and scratched down the middle.

Austin hissed then slammed his mouth down on hers, his cock still spearing her. She was almost out of breath when he released her lips and shouted before his cum filled her.

Kiley caressed every piece of available skin. The muscles in his shoulders flexed as he pulled out and collapsed on the floor beside her.

"Thank God this is thick carpet. I'm too damn old to be doing this on the floor," he mumbled.

"No, you're not." She giggled while rolling to curve into him. He'd just proved his ability to rock her world in the best way.

Austin chuckled and the lighthearted sound made her grin wider. She couldn't ever remember having so much fun in her life. A series of one-night stands then a friends-with-benefits arrangement with Gray had been all she'd ever experienced after she'd been set free.

She'd suspected for a while that Gray wanted more from her, but Kiley hadn't felt that deep longing for him she'd thought only existed in movies. Now she knew differently. But instead of getting to lose herself and enjoy, she knew she needed to get up and do her job.

"I have to go downstairs," she said. "We never made cookies yesterday and I need to spend some time with Jesse."

"I know." He ran his hand down her arm. "I don't want to let you go."

Kiley laughed. "Don't you have meetings to attend to or something?"

"I do." Austin climbed to his feet before reaching and lifting her up, too. "We have to finish up with Tony because he's leaving today to heal at home."

She bent and scooped up her clothes while Austin readjusted his jeans. "He really is going to be okay, right?"

"Yes," Austin assured her. "We also need to decide what to do about the attacks."

"I can't believe this is all happening." She busied herself with dressing and did not look at him. "I can understand why the Council wants to go public, but it scares me."

Austin grasped her arm to pull her around to face him. "It should scare you—it terrifies me, but the pros do outweigh the cons. However, I don't think it's the right decision for everyone. Some need the shadows. The comfort of Pack without being in the spotlight. I'm glad the Packs have the choice whether or not they want to go public."

She wanted to know but wasn't sure how to ask what Austin would do.

"Tyler will be going public. He lost several members of his old Pack to hunters and that was one of the reasons he left the area. They're safe here, but he still lives with the regret and pain of not being able to keep them safe. He needs to do this."

Kiley nodded.

"But my Pack is different. We won't be coming out. It's not what we need."

She sucked in a sharp breath.

"I've spoken to my advisors, inner circle and every single member of the Pack. It's not what is right for us. Plus, I will be opening my home to those who leave their Packs because they don't want to be in the open. There will be some shuffling of Pack members, but it will all work out."

Kiley actually felt better than she had since hearing about the Council's plan.

"We can talk more about this later, if you want," Austin said.

"I think I'd like that," she replied.

"Good." He kissed her gently. "Let's get our days started so we can come back here tonight."

* * * *

Jesse threw the tennis ball, laughing to see the puppy, Daisy, scrambling after it. Kiley watched from her seat on the grass only a few feet away. Jesse threw the ball a dozen or so more times. Finally, she grew tired and ran over to fall into Kiley's lap. Laughing, Kiley caught her. Daisy barreled in after the little girl.

She couldn't resist tightening her arms around Jesse.

The pup meant so much to her and Kiley had a feeling she wouldn't have many more days like this. The uncomplicated life she'd been living was changing.

"I love my puppy!" Jesse exclaimed.

"She is a very good puppy," Kiley agreed. "And I know you'll take really good care of her."

"I will!" Jesse promised.

Daisy nipped at the bottom of Jesse's pants, let go, then did it again, barking the entire time. Jesse giggled and tried to catch her, but each time the dog backed away and barked again.

"Silly Daisy," Jesse told her new pup.

She said it so seriously Kiley couldn't contain her grin. Jesse was such a sweet girl. The love she had for her tiny pet was obvious. She would probably follow in her dad's footsteps someday. Jesse would make a great leader.

"Do you think Daisy can swim?" Jesse asked a minute later when Daisy had finally settled down on the grass next to them.

"Well, some dogs like water. I think I heard Labs especially do," Kiley told her. "Do you want to go in and put your swimsuit on? We could find out."

"Really?" Jesse jumped up. "That would be so cool."

Jesse hopped around on the spot, causing Daisy to bark and bounce around, too.

Kiley shook her head in amusement. "Okay, swimming it is."

They headed toward the house, but several feet away, Daisy growled, stopping in place.

"Daisy?" Jesse asked and took a step toward the pup.

Kiley caught her hand. "Hold on, honey." There had to be a reason the dog had started acting up. "I'll get her." When she stooped to pick up the puppy, Daisy took off too quickly for Kiley to reach for her.

"Daisy! Daisy!" Jesse called after her in a panic.

"It's okay, sweetheart, she won't go far." Kiley tried to calm the screaming girl. Jesse threw herself around, trying to break loose from Kiley's hold.

"But she doesn't know her way home. What if she goes too far and gets lost?" Jesse asked, tears in her eyes.

Well, damn, she couldn't let Daisy go astray. Kiley waved at one of the guards on the back porch. He walked over but kept his eyes focused and scanning the area. Todd was one of the younger guards and she knew he was related to Tyler in some way. It might have been by marriage—Kiley wasn't one hundred percent sure. But she did know he wouldn't let anything happen to Jesse. She still heard Daisy barking and she needed to catch the dog before she got too far.

When Todd reached them, she smiled. "Would you take Jesse up to her room? Daisy got away from us and I need to go after her."

"Of course I can take Jesse, but what about you?" he asked in concern.

"I want to go with you," Jesse said loudly.

"I will be right back, Jesse. I'm sure your daddy wouldn't want you hiking through the woods right now. But you can see pretty far from your bedroom window. So why don't you watch for me from there? That way you can keep an eye out and see when I bring Daisy to you again," she suggested.

Jesse thought about it for several moments. "Fine." She shrugged, finally agreeing.

Kiley bent down and kissed her cheek. "Thank you. You be good now."

She was about to turn and head off when Todd spoke again, "Ms. Kiley, I really don't think Alpha Tyler or Alpha Austin would like you going by yourself, either."

Kiley looked up at him "I'm a big girl and this is what I'm here for. I won't be wandering around putting myself in danger. I'm only going to get the dog."

He didn't look convinced, but Kiley smiled at him, then swung around and set off in the direction Daisy had run. It wasn't difficult to follow the scent trail. The dog hadn't been in this part of the territory before, so her scent was easy to pick up without having to distinguish old from new. She could also still hear Daisy, which was good because there'd be no way she'd be returning to the house without the dog. Kiley glanced over her shoulder and saw Jesse at her bedroom window, waving. She waved back then returned to her mission.

She kept going north, and after a while Daisy's bark got closer. She wasn't too far from the house when she cut off the path and found the puppy. Daisy danced around and Kiley growled at the little thing. "Stupid dog," she mumbled, scooping the pet up.

That was when she saw them. Several sets of footprints next to four paw prints. Kiley bent down to get a better look, making sure she had a good hold of the small creature. The footprints were pretty fresh. She closed her eyes and concentrated on the area surrounding her. It didn't seem likely that Tyler would have any guards out this far merely to watch the house. No, this was someone who wasn't supposed to be there. The imprints were deep, which made her think whoever had made them had watched the house for a long time, too. She shivered at the unease traveling down her spine.

Standing and turning in a slow circle, Kiley held Daisy more tightly against her chest. She felt no danger around her, but even so a small part of her had begun to panic. While she could still see the house, there was no way she would be detected in the thick brush. There was the lingering scent of a shifter — not one she knew. And she had no idea when the stranger would return.

Kiley jumped when a rustle of leaves came from behind her. She darted a look around. She still didn't see or sense anyone, but she had had enough.

Without looking over her shoulder, she took off toward the house. She cradled Daisy as best she could so the little dog wouldn't be jostled around too much. The poor thing was whimpering.

She slipped, scraping her leg on a rock, but it didn't slow

her down. The panic remained, but it was also accompanied by an urgency to get to safety. The end of the path was coming up. She jumped over a fallen tree branch and stumbled a little when she landed poorly. It didn't even hurt, with the adrenaline pumping through her body. Now Kiley just needed to reach the back door.

Austin watched Tyler accept a handshake from Lamont then Cain. Tyler had told Austin already that he would announce the Pack's presence so there was no surprise for Austin. Tyler and Austin had spoken long and honestly about what they were going to do. They'd supported each other even though they were taking different paths. Tyler's was the sixth Pack to agree. Things were moving along quickly and it wouldn't be long until the Council actually went through with the action of bringing the shifters into the world for real.

Lamont turned to him and held his hand out. "Thank you, Austin. I appreciate everything you're doing."

Austin felt a little guilty at not being able to give Lamont the answer the older Alpha probably wanted. "I'm sorry, Alpha, but..."

Lamont squeezed his hand. "There is no need to apologize. I respect your decision. This move isn't for everyone. We understand that. And your willingness to take members of Packs who don't want to be public is wonderful. I hope we find more Alphas like you."

Austin relaxed, just a little. "Thank you, Alpha."

Lamont dipped his head. "You are an extremely good Alpha. I have no doubt your Pack will flourish in the next few years."

Lamont released his hand and Austin couldn't hide his grin. "I believe so."

Cain, who was never one for formality, didn't shake his hand. They'd been friends for too long, both once Betas of their Packs, until Austin had taken over his and become Alpha. Cain wrapped his big arms around Austin's waist and lifted him off his feet in a strong bear hug.

"I like your girl," Cain said quietly. "Make sure you take care of her."

"She's not my girl," Austin said. "Yet."

"She will be," Cain told him.

Austin pounded on the other man's back until he was released. He knew Cain had found true happiness with his mate, Emily. Austin hoped the same would be said about him soon. "I look forward to being as happy as you," Austin told his friend.

Cain smirked and opened his mouth to respond, when Austin picked up panic and desperation. The feelings were so strong Austin struggled to catch his breath. The way the others in the room stiffened told Austin he wasn't the only one who'd noticed the strong emotions.

"Kiley." Austin whispered her name.

Without a thought for anyone else, Austin raced from the room. He caught Lamont saying something about a mate, but he was already in the hallway. He sped to the back door, his wolf telling him Kiley was that way. Austin scanned with all his senses for any sign of danger, but he couldn't find any. Yet he sensed Kiley's fear as strongly as though his heart beat in time with hers. He passed a couple of guards but didn't slow down. He heard the others behind him and that made him feel a little calmer, but until he saw Kiley, nothing would be okay.

Austin yanked the sliding glass door to the side so hard it shook. Kiley sprinted across the yard with Jesse's new puppy in her arms. He leapt off the deck and hit the grass moving. He ran at full speed, until she jumped into the air and he had to stop to catch her. He wrapped his arms around her, cushioning her fall to the ground. He hit the floor, but he cradled her and the dog she carried. His breath whooshed out of him as she panted, "Someone is watching the house."

He didn't hesitate but rolled her over onto her back and covered her body with his. The puppy she held wiggled around, but there was no way he'd let her up until he knew she was safe. Austin lifted his head and Gray, Colt and Cain all took off in the direction Kiley had come from. The air around them swirled and he knew they had shifted.

It didn't take long for the howl from Colt, telling him it was safe for now.

When Austin was sure there was no immediate danger to Kiley, he finally took the time to look her over. Her cheeks were flushed from her run, but she was starting to calm down. However, she hadn't released her hold on the dog, or him. He glimpsed a shadow and looked up to see Tyler watching him. Tyler held out a hand to help him up, but Austin shook his head. He couldn't let go of Kiley yet. He rolled off Kiley but remained holding her as he got to his feet. He pulled Kiley up with him and held her elbow to check for injuries.

"You okay?" Tyler asked her.

She nodded but allowed Austin to keep the embrace. He was grateful—he needed to see for himself she was unharmed.

"I'm sorry," she said, blushing, her voice cracking a little. "When I realized someone was watching the house…how close they were to Jesse, I panicked a little."

"It's okay, baby," Austin tried to soothe. It was so apparent she cared deeply for the little girl.

"There's nothing to be embarrassed about, Kiley," Tyler added. "My daughter is the most precious thing in the world to me. I would have done the same."

"I doubt that," Kiley mumbled.

Austin ignored her comment. He would talk to her later about being so hard on herself. Right now, though, she needed to be taken care of. "You're bleeding," he told her lightly. He didn't want to make a big deal about it, but the wolf smelled her blood and he was furious. "Let's get you inside and cleaned up."

She limped to the house.

"What the hell is wrong with your foot?" he demanded.

Kiley froze. When she glanced at him, she was frowning. "I must have twisted my ankle. It's no big deal."

Austin almost exploded. He growled low, managing to keep most of his anger in. Tyler stepped over and took Daisy out of Kiley's arms. It was a good thing, too, because a second later Austin had Kiley scooped up and was stalking his way across the yard. He made sure his hold was firm but wouldn't hurt. He would get her all patched up, then they were going to talk. The back door was still open, so he didn't pause in entering the house. He didn't realize he was still growling until Kiley put her hand over his heart.

"Your eyes are glowing," she said, quietly.

He wasn't surprised. His wolf was closer now than usual. He hadn't been this upset in a very long time. He didn't respond, instead carefully taking each step up the stairs. His room was the farthest down the hall. He carried her, stopping long enough to open the door then slam it behind them. Austin set her gently on the bed and turned to pace away from her. On his third pass, she tried to speak.

"Austin—"

He held up a hand, stopping her. He needed a few minutes. Luckily, she seemed to understand, since she remained silent. When he thought he had regained control, he stood in front of her, looking down.

She met his gaze for only a moment before looking away.

"Look at me," he ground out between clenched teeth. When she did, he nodded his approval. "I will never hurt you. Or allow anyone else to. But I am an Alpha and smelling your blood is hard to handle."

"It's not something I'm used to. You know, someone caring if I get hurt."

"Well, get used to it," he responded. "Since you seem incapable of staying out of trouble."

Kiley opened her mouth, snapped it closed, opened it again. No words came out. Austin almost laughed, it was so comical. He liked being able to surprise her.

Austin was going to really throw her with his next words.

"From now on, I'm in charge of your body, since you seem to think it's okay to abuse it."

"My body?" she repeated slowly.

Austin nodded. "Yes, now take off your pants."

"Take off my pants?" she echoed with a grin. "Well, why didn't you ask sooner?"

Austin chuckled as she scrambled to her knees. She put her fingers on her jean button but paused.

"Now, are you sure you want just my pants off?" she teased.

Austin liked this part of their connection. When they were alone, Kiley seemed so much more relaxed and she flirted with him. The remaining anger drained from him. If she was in a playful mood, he would take advantage of it. In fact, he had a pretty good idea.

"You're right. You might have other injuries. Go ahead and undress completely," he agreed.

Kiley held in a laugh, but she was obviously struggling with it. Her bright eyes were shining and he hoped he'd be able to take away her fear from earlier. If he could give her a little bit of peace, to let her know that others, cared about her, then he would be happy.

His hard cock strained against the zipper of his jeans, but he ignored his own need. This was about her. She did what he'd asked until she lay in front of him bare. Austin scratched his chin, faking deep thought.

"Turn around so I can check for more injuries."

Kiley sighed but did as he requested, making out she'd only given in for his benefit. She jumped when he ran his hands over her lower back and down. Then she trembled.

"Okay, come on," he said and helped her turn to face him again.

She took the hand he offered. Austin helped her from the bed, quickly leading her into the attached bathroom. He lifted her and set her on the vanity. He walked over to the large standing shower and turned on the water.

"Uh, Austin," she called to him.

Austin didn't respond, instead testing the temperature then returning to her. "Now, let's see," he said and took her ankle gently in his hands.

"It's already better," she told him.

He believed her, since shifters healed very quickly. "My body, remember?" he told her with mock sternness. "I'll tell you when it's better."

Kiley rolled her eyes but did let Austin run his hands over her ankle before he picked up a washcloth and got it wet. He cleaned her foot, her knee, all the scrapes she'd picked up. He enjoyed caring for her.

"There now, all better," he said, placing a kiss on her once-hurt ankle. "I never want to see blood on your precious skin again."

She nodded.

Austin released her foot then drew her close to his chest. They kissed, slowly and deeply.

"Now let me wash this body of mine," he murmured, pulling her off the counter toward the hot water.

He pushed her gently in and began taking off his clothes. Austin stepped inside to join her and she reached out, grabbing his shoulders. Kiley kissed him this time and he responded hungrily, devouring her mouth, his mind clouding.

"I need to feel you. I need you inside me," she begged.

"Yes, love...yes."

Austin lifted her and she wrapped her legs around his waist. He placed her back against the cool tile of the shower before he lined his cock up at her entrance.

Kiley sighed as he filled her, causing the feeling of completion and contentment to rush through him. Austin moved slowly, stretching her until he was buried deep. He growled and pulled out slightly to thrust again. He fucked her hard against the shower wall, making Kiley grip the tiles for support. Her nails pierced his flesh and the sting felt right. As though she was marking him.

The sound of flesh slapping flesh and their moans filled

the room. Kiley met each one of his strokes. She was strong and powerful on her own, but when they came together, it felt as if they were burning from the inside out. She clamped down on his cock almost painfully. He grunted and she threw back her head and howled, reaching completion.

"We're not done," Austin told her through gritted teeth and plunged in and out again, each time faster and harder.

"That's it," she encouraged. "Take me…do what you want with me. Make me yours…"

That was the best thing Austin had ever heard. But when she tilted her head to the side to show her submission to him, he was in Heaven. At that moment, they were in perfect sync.

"Fuck!" he cried out, slamming into her hard before coming. His vision darkened and he had to slap his hand against the hard tile to hold himself and Kiley up.

"That was incredible," she panted, hot against his neck.

"Damn," Austin mumbled. "My legs are numb."

"My entire body is tingling," she said.

Austin peered down at her and they both laughed. He grasped her hip tightly then carefully withdrew from her. After he'd pulled from her body, Austin made sure Kiley was steady on her feet before he grabbed the bar of soap.

"Let's get cleaned up and downstairs," Austin said. "One of these days, I'm going to cuddle with you after we make love."

"Yeah," Kiley said. "I sure the hell hope so."

Chapter Five

Austin lifted his head from the pillow at the soft knock on his bedroom door. Beside him, Kiley remained sound asleep. The rest of the day had been fairly calm, considering how the morning had started. They'd kept Jesse inside, which had not made the little girl happy, but they had to keep her safe. Everyone had turned in early so Tony, Cain and Lamont could leave at dawn. A glance at the nightstand clock showed Austin that it was still the middle of the night.

He climbed carefully off the bed. He smelled Colt in the hall and sensed his Beta's frustration. Something else must have happened. Austin opened up but put his finger to his lips so Colt would wait. Silently, he closed the door and gestured farther down the hall. Colt didn't even blink at his Alpha being naked in front of him. They shared a cabin at home and ran together in wolf form often, so they'd seen each other nude more than a time or two. Still, some of Colt's unease left, to be replaced with amusement. Austin didn't mind. He was proud of his time with Kiley. It didn't bother him in the least if others knew what they had been doing. He enjoyed having Kiley's scent all over him.

"We found an abandoned SUV just inside the city limits. It carried the same scent as Tony's attacker, but it's different from the one Kiley found behind the house," Colt told him.

"You think he left town?" Austin asked, although he knew the answer.

"Wouldn't make sense for him to leave. I think he wants us to think that." Colt confirmed Austin's suspicion.

Austin nodded. "I agree."

"We found a cheap motel a couple miles down the road.

We think he stayed there for a couple of weeks. He would have been there when we arrived—"

"Someone knew about the meetings as soon as we scheduled them. They've been watching us for a while."

"I think it's because of Tony. Tony said he felt he'd been followed a few times, going from Pack to Pack. He could never pinpoint exactly where or who, just more of a feeling," Colt continued. "He's going to be the most public figure, the face of shifters, and someone doesn't want him to be that."

"We need to get him out of town."

"Lamont is already on it. The Council is sending two guards down to escort Tony back home. From there, the Council will contact him on the next steps."

It made sense to get Tony out of there, but Austin worried that would be real work. "He'll only be followed again. Tyler's Pack will be safe, but Tony's won't be."

"I know," Colt agreed. "I tried to talk to Tony about it, but he says they have precautions in their territory that aren't set up here. He wouldn't give me details, but he seems to believe he'll be safer."

"You don't agree?"

"I think he'd be safer if we caught the shifters after him," Colt said.

Austin studied his Beta. Colt was good at his job, but they were much more than just Alpha and second. Colt was his brother in everything but blood. The emotions Colt tried to hide were bleeding through, though, and Austin didn't know how to help his best friend. "Does he feel the same way about you?" Austin asked gently.

Colt lowered his head. "I don't know."

Fuck, Colt's bisexuality had never been a big deal to him, but it had caused issues previously with lovers. For some reason, the partners who Colt chose believed because he was attracted to both men and women, Colt had commitment issues or was a slut. That couldn't have been further from the truth, however. Colt loved with all his heart and even though he'd been hurt time and time again, he was open to finding real love. If Tony couldn't or wouldn't give Colt what he deserved, he wasn't good enough for his best friend. "Colt—"

"I know." Colt held up his hand. "But I'm in love with him. And I can't let him leave here without doing everything I can to protect him."

Austin sighed. Once Colt had made up his mind about something, there was no changing it. "Let me get dressed and we'll head out and see what we can hunt up."

Colt snapped his head up. "No! I mean, I want permission to go, but I don't want to take you away from Kiley."

"She'll understand. And you're not going alone. Ten minutes, and I'll meet you out by the truck."

"Thanks, Austin." Colt gripped his shoulder.

"Ten minutes." Austin turned away and strolled to his room. Hopefully, he wouldn't wake Kiley and would be able to sneak out again. He pushed the door open slowly and crept inside.

"Why are you sneaking in?"

She didn't sound angry, merely sleepy.

"Colt needed to talk to me," he explained.

"Then come to bed," she said, rolling over.

The soft rustle of the sheets reminded him of what they'd done under them hours ago. His cock began to harden, but he ignored it.

"I can't. I have to help Colt with something."

More movement from the bed, then she switched on the lamp. "What's going on?" she asked.

"They found the SUV and the motel where the shifter who was around when Tony got shot has been staying," Austin explained, reaching down to pick up his discarded jeans. "Colt wants to do some more hunting for the suspect and I don't want him to go alone."

"Austin?"

"Hmm?" He needed to find his shirt and his shoes. He should have a backpack somewhere, too.

"Austin!"

He whirled around. "What?"

"Why were you standing in the hall naked?"

Austin looked at her in surprise. "Because, darling, Colt knocked on the door and I didn't want to waste time having to dress then undress again to get back in bed with you."

"That's a good answer," she said. "Now what's going on?"

He chuckled. As he walked to the bed where his very rumpled and beautiful lover lay, all Austin really wanted to do was climb in with her again. But he wouldn't leave Colt out on his own. "Colt wants to go and try to find the shifters from earlier. Cain called off the search and they're leaving in the morning after the Council guards get here, when they'll escort Tony home safely."

"Colt can't go by himself." She rubbed at her eyes. "That's not safe."

Fuck, she was adorable. "That's why I'm getting dressed."

"Oh." Kiley shook her head. "Of course." She pushed the covers off before standing.

"What are you doing?"

"Getting dressed. Neither you nor Colt know the city. I'll be helpful."

While she had a point, Austin didn't want her anywhere near the threat. "Uh…"

"I'm going with you," she said. "Don't even try to argue."

He blew out a breath, calculating his chances of not starting a fight.

"I'm going," she said, more firmly.

Austin watched her quickly pull on her clothes. He wanted to protect Kiley. She'd been through so much in her life, but on the other hand, she was strong. "Just don't get hurt," he ordered, strolling to her. He grasped her chin. "Remember this body belongs to me."

She rolled her eyes in response. "Sure, and Austin?"

"Yeah, babe?"

"Next time put some damn clothes on."

"You got it." He kissed her once more, fast but hard, then resumed collecting his own belongings.

They moved quickly until they were sneaking out of the front door. Austin knew he'd be able to tell Tyler what they were doing, but he didn't want to worry his friend. This was to help Colt and Tony. If they didn't return with a better lead on the shifters, he'd confess what they had done. If they were able to actually capture at least one of the shifters, then Tony would be safer.

"Hey, Kiley," Colt greeted her softly. "Thanks for coming."

"I'm happy to help," she told him. "Where's the last place you caught the scent?"

"We found the vehicle at the edge of the county line. The scent circles the vehicles and goes out for miles."

"They backtracked," Kiley guessed.

"Can we discuss this in the vehicle?" Tony asked, joining them. "I don't know how long we have until Cain realizes I'm not asleep."

"What are you doing here?" Colt asked, racing to Tony's side. "You should be resting."

Tony snorted. "I'm rested enough. I'm okay, really."

Not wanting to intrude, Austin grasped Kiley's elbow and led her to the passenger side of the black SUV. She didn't resist and in fact smiled at him before climbing in and closing the door. He walked around to get behind the wheel as Colt and Tony continued to talk. He couldn't *not* hear what they were saying, but at least giving them the illusion of privacy was respectful.

It was only a few minutes until Colt and Tony were getting into the back seat. Austin didn't waste any time starting the vehicle and reversing out of the drive. "Where to?"

"Not far," Kiley answered.

"Do you know something?" Colt leaned forward between the seats.

"I've been thinking about where I found the tracks watching the house. None of the rotations found any sign of anyone, but we know someone got inside the territory. When I was a kid—" She squeezed her hands together and Austin placed one of his over hers in comfort. "There's an old trail that some of us found and that we kept secret."

"A trail?" Austin asked gently. "How young were you?"

"Five or six?" she responded. "Riker hadn't..."

Austin lifted her palm and kissed her wrist. The support helped to settle her.

"Anyway," she said. "It's a tricky trail and the Alpha at the time blocked it off so no one would get hurt. Some of the teenagers would get curious and dare one another to take it, but Larry finally convinced them it was too dangerous even for that. As far as I know, most of the Pack has forgotten about it, but it would still be there. It also leads right to the section of the territory where I saw the tracks."

"Holy shit," Colt said.

"I should have remembered about it earlier."

"You thought of it now," Austin told her.

"It's a long shot, but I thought we'd start there."

"Any other reason you think the shifters might be there?" Tony questioned.

"The trail starts about five miles from where the SUV was abandoned."

"It's a solid lead," Colt said excitedly.

"Tony, duck down," Austin ordered. He waved at one of the guards at the gate, who motioned him through. They were used to Austin coming and going, so that shouldn't be unusual. If the guards didn't spot Tony, who was supposed to be under the protection of his family, their group wouldn't get stopped.

"Take a right," Kiley told him.

Austin followed the curve of the gravel road for several minutes before Kiley let go of his hand and pointed.

"Just up ahead you're going to see a walking path. Pull over next to it. We'll be on foot from there," she said. "It would be easier if we shifted."

Austin felt the jump in his pulse. *Am I going to get to*

shift with Kiley? The night seemed to be getting better and better. It was going to be very interesting to see how his wolf reacted to Kiley's. The trailhead Kiley had told him about came into view and if he hadn't been looking for it, Austin would have passed right on by. The entire area was overgrown with weeds and roughage. Austin pulled off to the side and parked the SUV, letting his lights shine over the path.

"Someone's been here," Kiley said, leaning forward to stare out of the windshield. "Some of the weeds are pushed down."

Austin squinted. She was right. "Let's go."

"Right behind you," Colt said.

Kiley was already out of the vehicles and crouched over the downed vegetation before he could. "I can smell them," she said when he stepped up beside her.

"Me, too. Smells recent, too."

Behind them, Colt and Tony were talking quietly, but it looked as though they were getting ready to shift.

"We should do this before something else happens," Kiley said, rising.

"Is everything going to be okay with you shifting? I know you don't do it often," Austin asked in a whisper.

"Sure." She shrugged and didn't sound convincing at all.

He took her hand in his. "Look at me," he ordered. Austin waited until she met his gaze. "I can take Colt and Tony with me and you don't have to go at all. I want you to be safe."

"No. I can do this. Plus, I wasn't kidding about the trail being dangerous. I need to show you the safest way."

Austin didn't like it, but he didn't want to hold Kiley back, either. Maybe this was what she needed, even if she was scared. If she faced the demons in her past, then she'd hopefully be able to move forward with him. "Okay, you undress in the SUV and we'll stay out here."

She sent him an amused look.

"I know you can shift with us, but I don't really want

anyone else to see you," Austin admitted.

"I'm pretty sure Tony and Colt only have eyes for each other."

"Not the point," Austin growled. He stepped forward to brush his body against hers. "Call me jealous, but this body" — he ran his hand under the hem of her shirt — "is all mine."

She shivered but smiled. "What if I don't want anyone to see you?"

Austin laughed. "As you recall, Colt has already seen me naked tonight."

Kiley growled, then pushed him away. "Smartass." But she did give him a quick peck on his check. With a wide grin, she strode over to his vehicle. She left the back door open, but he saw the outline of her pulling her shirt off.

"Ready?" he called over to Tony and Colt, who were still standing off to the side and not looking at Kiley.

"Yes, Alpha," Colt said.

Austin walked over while yanking his shirt over his head. Tony turned away but began to undress too. With shifters, being naked was not unusual. Most times, shifters would remove their clothes because when they transformed, they could get tangled up in the cloth if the fabric hadn't already ripped. Still, it was polite to give the maximum amount of perceived privacy possible.

Austin kept his gaze out to the land they were going to explore. He wanted to watch Kiley, but this wasn't the right time. He'd make sure they got another chance to run together, but hopefully they would be alone the next time.

Once naked, Austin crouched down in the weeds and closed his eyes. He called forward his wolf to take over. The transformation rolled over him in waves and within a minute, he stood on all four paws. Austin stretched out his neck before looking around him.

In his wolf form, the world appeared so different to him.

The sounds of the area surrounding him were louder and sharper. He swiveled his ears forward to try to pick up any movement that might be close by. While the scent of shifters was fairly recent, the trace was at least a couple of hours old. There was no other evidence anyone else had been in the area.

A crunch of leaves behind him had Austin turning and he saw Tony and Colt had finished their own shifts. As an Alpha, it was easier and quicker for him to change. The longer it'd been or if the shifter tried to fight the transformation, it could become painful and last several minutes.

He trotted over to where Kiley was still inside the vehicle. Austin came around to the door slowly, trying to hear if she was having any problems. Before he'd glimpsed into the interior, something leapt out and landed on him.

They rolled and he immediately caught Kiley's scent. Once they stopped, he hovered over her while she panted up at him. The brightness in her eyes made him feel good. The happiness coming off her surprised him. He knew she didn't shift often because of her past with Riker, but she seemed to enjoy it. He lowered his head and licked at her muzzle.

Kiley whimpered then squirmed out from under him. Once on her feet, she darted forward and nipped his leg prior to backing off again. She wriggled her entire body. He pounced in retaliation, but she moved out of the way fast. As she jogged off, Austin followed behind.

Colt and Tony were much more subdued. Colt was lying down while Tony groomed him. It was sweet and romantic, but Austin preferred the playfulness of Kiley. She made circles, kicking up debris and dirt.

He caught her shoulder and pushed her off balance. If she could have laughed in wolf form, Austin was pretty sure she would have.

Tony rose and walked toward them with Colt by his side. Austin lifted his head and even though he would have rather played with Kiley, they needed to get to the search. He nosed her in the direction of the trail and she grew serious.

Kiley shook her entire body hard before dipping her head once and walking briskly toward the trail. Austin fell in step behind her with Colt after him and Tony last.

She made no noise stepping over broken branches and dead foliage. If they got the chance to hunt, he'd be very interested in what she'd be able to do. The way Kiley moved her body and only stopped to listen or scent spoke of former training. He wasn't sure he wanted to know what Riker had done to her that Kiley tracked so well, but it came in handy right then.

His rear paw slipped on the crumbling soil of the ledge and he scrambled to catch himself as she lurched around and grabbed hold of his scruff. He hadn't really been in danger of falling, but her panic had both of them breathing fast.

Austin made a sound in the back of his throat to hopefully reassure her. Kiley released her hold on him, but instead of moving away, she lowered her snout until it was under his chin. He didn't know if she was worried she'd hurt him or if she needed comfort. Since he needed to soothe whatever was wrong, he rubbed his muzzle all over her face until she had calmed.

It was at times like these Austin wished shifters shared the mental bond or whatever other purely fictional telepathic connection movies and books gave them. All Austin could work with was what vibes she gave off and everything he picked up said Kiley was afraid.

It took all her mental strength for Kiley to back away from Austin once she'd gotten his reassurance that he was okay. God, she hated this old fucking path. Austin seemed fine, but his stumble had scared her badly. Her heart beat so hard that drowned out all other noises at that moment. His caresses helped and she took deep breaths until she was in control once again.

Colt and Tony were looking around them as if they were

keeping an eye out, but she had the feeling they were giving her time to collect herself. Now she knew Austin really was uninjured, Kiley faced front again.

They gotten at least halfway down the trail and she had to get them through the rest of the way. Up ahead was the most dangerous terrain. It was a good thing their shifter sight was better than their human, because they were going to need it.

Kiley stepped forward carefully.

There was no light around them and the trees in the area blocked any illumination they would have gotten from the moon. While it wasn't pitch-black, it was close enough. A shiver racked her body, but she wasn't going to wuss out now.

As Kiley led the way, she had to watch the broken rocks to make sure no one cut their paws open.

It was slow going and had to have taken more than half an hour, but climbing higher and higher, she was beyond relieved. Up here, at least some of the moon beams shone. Kiley stepped to the side when Austin, Colt and Tony finished the trek. The view from the top was beautiful.

Austin's hard body pressed up against her and she leaned into his solid form. It felt good they'd made it that far and the danger was behind them. Of course, if they returned down the same way, they'd be in trouble. Maybe she'd convince Austin to run to the house instead and they could take another vehicle to pick up his. Yeah, that would be best. She did not want to set foot on that path again.

While Austin peered around the territory, Kiley took the opportunity to scout the closest area. She already knew how beautiful it was up there, but she felt no connection to it. The territory might be a part of her, but she didn't love it.

Maybe that was what was wrong with her.

Her inability to bond with the land and people had kept her from feeling at home in the place. She'd suffered too much trauma there. It saddened her to realize she wasn't going to make a home there ever again. In the back of her mind, she'd thought one day she'd be healed and would return to the Pack. It was one reason why she did the small jobs for Tyler and hung around the others. Why she'd taken the chance to get to know little Jesse. But now she suspected her future didn't lie in this territory.

Kiley jumped when Austin pushed his nose against her side. She'd been so lost in thought she hadn't realized he'd joined her. She wanted to turn into his warm body and weep, but she wouldn't. It wasn't his responsibility to take care of her. He barely knew her. While the connection between them was powerful, Kiley had nothing to offer him. She didn't even have a past she'd be able to tell him about. Kiley *wouldn't*, anyway.

He nudged her again and she was glad to be in her wolf form. Kiley couldn't talk and that probably saved her from making a fool of herself.

Colt trotted over to them and Kiley motioned her head to indicate they should be going. They needed to track down the shifters who had left the scent ahead of them. Colt nodded, turning around to get Tony while Austin still watched her. She knew he had a lot of questions after probably picking up on her emotions, but that needed to wait.

Once Colt and Tony rejoined them, Kiley attempted to lead off again, but Austin easily brushed her aside to get up front. Yeah, she was surprised he'd let her go first so long to begin with, so she wasn't shocked. She fell in step behind him and watched him stalk through the forest, all broad shoulders and long, lean body. He was a very handsome wolf, with his light fur and smooth muscles. Kiley had seen a few Alphas, but none of them had had Austin's gorgeous looks. Even though Tyler was a very good-looking man, Austin was the one who she thought of as perfect.

She watched his strong back, meaning when he paused, Kiley almost ran into him.

It was quiet, so she didn't know if he'd spotted something, but she didn't want to move and ruin whatever he was up to. Behind her, both Colt and Tony had frozen, too. Out of the corner of her eye, she saw them look around. Austin lowered his body to the ground slowly and they all followed suit. Kiley still couldn't determine what was up.

As she lay on the cool damp ground, she took a deep breath and realized the scents they'd been following had intensified. And were only a couple of minutes old.

They'd caught up with the felines.

Great, now what are we going to do? Kiley realized they hadn't made a plan on how to deal with the felines. Austin turned his head and their gazes met. He was planning something and she couldn't read what he wanted. He started to crawl backward until he was at her side. Then his body shimmied and he transformed to human once more.

Kiley watched him, mesmerized. He shifted so seamlessly. It had taken her several minutes to become a wolf. She wasn't sure she'd make the change so soon after her first one.

"There are three of them up ahead watching the house," he whispered close to her ear. With their targets being shifters, Kiley knew he had to be careful not to be overheard. "You stay in wolf form in case you have to run them down. You know the territory better than us and where they might take off to."

She nodded her agreement then he went to speak to Colt and Tony. Kiley listened to him explaining his plan to the two men. He and Colt would go in human form while she and Tony would stay in their animal forms. Tony was still weak and recovering so it would also be hard for him to transform again. Austin knew their limitations and was forming his plan around them.

Colt shifted before dragging forward the backpack he'd been carrying with him. Kiley hadn't thought about it until she saw Colt pulling out clothes and passing them over to Austin. Obviously, Austin was prepared. It made Kiley wonder how many times the two had done things like this. He and Colt dressed silently and Austin came right next to her again.

"Cover this side," he told her. "Tony will take east, Colt west, and I'll walk up on them from the north. I'll let them see me and we'll find out how they react. I expect them to run."

Once again, all she could do was nod, although she wanted to tell him to be careful. They didn't know what these shifters were capable of and they'd already shot Tony. They might still have a weapon.

"It's okay," he told her, running his palm down her back. "I'll be careful and there are four of us and three of them."

But what about the weapons? she wanted to demand.

"If they come at you, use whatever you have to. Teeth, claws, anything you have to," he said.

Kiley raised her paw and laid it on his knee. She would do her job and make sure their targets didn't get away. They wouldn't be hurting anyone else.

Austin kissed the top of her head before he snuck away. Kiley looked around her and saw that both Colt and Tony had already disappeared. No doubt getting into position. She remained low to the ground while creeping forward until she had the three felines in sight.

As unprepared as her group had been to come across the three felines, they didn't seem to be worried about being discovered. Here they were in a Wolf Pack territory and they were sitting around a tree watching the Alpha compound, talking and laughing. They had no idea they were being stalked. How stupid were these guys?

She spotted movement, then Austin came into view.

The minute the felines saw him, they stiffened and jumped up.

Kiley prepared herself to stop them if they ran in her direction.

"Gentlemen," Austin said clearly. "I hope you have a good excuse for being here."

Instead of answering, the three felines ran. In three different directions.

As soon as the young blond headed in her direction, Kiley rose before stalking forward. She was still hidden, but the feline was almost to her. She leapt out and blocked his path.

He skidded to a stop almost comically. He windmilled his arms, barely keeping on his feet.

She growled and snapped at him.

"Whoa." He held up his hands even as he took a step away.

Kiley snarled in warning. She would chase after him if she had to. Each step forward she took, he matched with one back. This close, she saw how very young he was. He couldn't have been older than nineteen or twenty. The odor of fear wafted off him in heavy waves.

There came a loud crash and howl of pain, but Kiley didn't take her eyes off her target. The noise had come from the direction where Tony had been, but it didn't resemble an animal sound so she hoped Tony was okay.

"Don't attack," the feline told her.

Kiley didn't plan on it unless he made her. She opened her mouth wide showing him her long canines.

"Drop down on your knees," Austin ordered, stepping behind the kid. "Hands behind your head."

The kid complied and Austin quickly tied the guy's hands.

"I'm going to check on Tony then Colt. Watch him," Austin ordered.

Kiley rumbled in response.

Austin chuckled and jogged off.

"Please," the feline chanted. "Please, please, please."

The words and tone were hauntingly familiar. She'd begged the same way this young man was now doing. Her heart and mind warred with each other. She wanted to show compassion, but she also knew her friends were still in danger.

She stopped snarling and instead took a guard position in front of the feline.

It seemed to take forever, but in reality, it was probably closer to twenty minutes before Austin, Colt, Tony and the other two felines were walking toward her. Kiley relaxed as Austin smiled at her then reached down to help the kid to his feet.

"Let's head to the compound."

Chapter Six

"What in the hell were you thinking?" Cain roared at Tony.

"Cain, calm down," Lamont said, placing a hand on his son's shoulder.

Austin watched as the young Enforcer took a deep breath. Cain wasn't the only person unhappy about them going off to investigate on their own—he was just the loudest.

"Where are the felines now?" Austin asked. They needed to get past the family drama and concentrate on the next steps.

"I have them locked up in the basement," Tyler said. "Riker had a jail down there and, while I've never used it, I figured now would be the first and only time it'll be necessary."

Fuck, Riker had been one sick puppy. What had he needed cells for? Austin looked over at his friend and saw Tyler was not proud of having to use the holding area, but they all knew he didn't have much of a choice.

"I put a call into the feline Prince," Tyler said. "I spoke with one of his family members and they promised the Prince would call me back. After we speak to him, we'll figure out what to do."

"I want to interrogate them," Cain demanded.

"That's not a good idea." They were the first words Tony had spoken since they'd all gathered in the living room.

They'd almost reached the door when Cain had come flying out, confronting his brother on Tony's disappearance. Apparently, Cain had woken up, seen Tony's note and woken the rest of the house to go find his brother. They'd brought the felines back before anyone had gone in search of Tony, luckily, but there were a lot of pissed-off shifters now.

"You know what else isn't a good idea?" Cain snapped. "Sneaking out and looking for trouble when you've been shot!"

"You seem to keep forgetting I'm a grown-ass man who can take care of myself," Tony argued. "You're not my Alpha, Cain, and you're not my boss!"

"How about I knock you on that grown ass?" Cain threatened.

"Enough!" Lamont didn't raise his voice, but the order was loud and clear.

Cain and Tony stepped away from one another.

"It's been a long night and we're all tired."

Cain and Tony nodded. Austin agreed with the older Alpha, too. He wanted this conversation over with so he could join Kiley upstairs. He'd sent her ahead of him to shower and get some sleep. He really wanted to join her in that bed.

"Now, we're not going to do anything until we hear back from the feline Prince," Lamont said. "I suggest we all head to bed for a few hours."

Tyler rose. It was his house, so even though Lamont had made his proposal, Tyler made the call. "I agree. It's going to be a long day. We need to get some shut-eye before we have to deal with our three guests."

Tony stood and Austin saw Colt watching him. It didn't appear that anyone else in the room noticed, though. Austin didn't know if Tony and Colt were hiding their relationship from those in the room, but with the sparks practically flying between them, he'd be surprised if the others didn't already know.

"I need a shower," Tony said, stomping out.

Colt glanced at Austin and Austin discreetly nodded to his Beta.

"I'm too old for this," Lamont mumbled. He, too, left.

Tyler smiled at him, next turning to Cain. "Nightcap?"

"Sure," Austin agreed while Cain nodded vigorously.

As Tyler strolled over to the small bar in the corner, Austin walked over to Cain.

"You okay, man?" Austin asked.

"Yeah." Cain ran his hands roughly over his face. "I didn't mean to yell at Tony. I've been so worried and now he's been shot."

Austin understood. If he were in Cain's situation, he'd probably have reacted very similarly. "He knows. Tony's tried and he wore himself out."

Cain dropped his hands and grinned at Austin. "You realize we're going to have to figure out a custody agreement for my brother, right?"

"Custody?" Austin asked.

"There's no way my dad's going to let Tony out of his sight for a while. I know you need your Beta, but I don't see how we'll separate those two," Cain said.

So, Cain knew about Tony and Colt's relationship and he seemed happy about it. "I think they'll let us know what they want to do," Austin replied, diplomatically.

Cain chuckled. "Yeah, they'll try."

Austin could only shake his head. Tony had a lot more responsibility than Colt, but Colt was loyal to Austin and the Pack. Austin would never stand in Colt's way, but he would hate to lose Colt as his Beta. He loved Colt like a brother.

Tyler joined them and handed each of them a crystal glass containing a small amount of brown liquid. He sniffed his drink. *Whiskey. Good whiskey.* He took a small sip and groaned in appreciation.

"That hits the spot," Cain said.

"So, Tony and Colt," Tyler mused. "I didn't see that coming."

"Oh, I did," Cain said. "The moment I arrived, I noticed that Tony couldn't keep his gaze off Colt. He is smitten."

Austin sure hoped so, since he knew Colt's feelings ran

deep.

"Lamont's going back home tomorrow," Cain said. "He's going to insist Tony joins him. I'm going to try to stay here until we can deal with the shifters."

Austin nodded. "If Colt wants to escort Tony to make sure he's safe, I'm okay with that."

"Good. I'll feel better knowing Colt's close by him."

"I'll talk to Colt in the morning. Make sure he knows it's okay with me."

"What about you?" Cain asked. "When are you heading off?"

Good question. With the threats and attack here at Tyler's, he didn't know how much the felines knew about him or his Pack. He was worried and, even if his inner circle assured him things were quiet, Austin was anxious to get home. But that meant leaving Kiley behind and he didn't know if he'd be capable of doing that.

"I can talk to her," Tyler said softly. He had to know what made Austin hesitate to answer Cain's question.

Austin shook his head. "I appreciate the offer, but I need to talk to her. If she doesn't want to come, then we'll work something out. I'm not giving up on the chance of having a relationship with her."

Cain slapped him on the back before he drained his glass. "That's the spirit. But why don't you just ask her to go with you temporarily?"

"What do you mean?" Austin questioned.

"It's obvious she's a caring person," Cain said. "You took in some of her former Pack. I'm sure there are things she could help you with. Bring her down for a few weeks to help with the Pack and in the meantime, you'll get to spend time with her."

That wasn't a terrible idea. Austin was doing his very best to bond with his new members, but he didn't know what they'd been through. He was taking care of them, but Austin hadn't experienced the same things they had. Kiley had not only gone through it, but worse. It might do both the Pack and her good to reconnect. If Kiley helped his Pack, she'd feel better about herself and Austin would be happy.

"I'll talk to her," Austin said. "See what she thinks about it."

"Good," Cain said, passing his empty glass to Tyler. "I'm going to hit the sack."

Tyler waited until Cain left to grip Austin's shoulder. "If you ask her to go, I think she will. Kiley wants to put what happened with Riker behind her and if she can help your Pack, that will allow her to finally do so."

"I don't want it to remind her of bad times," Austin said.

"I don't think it will. She's still living in the past and she needs to get beyond what happened. I know it won't be easy for her and she'll never forget, but I don't think she can heal here. I believe she can with you."

"I do need to get home," Austin commented. "I guess I'll talk to her in the morning, too."

"Good." Tyler gave him a one-armed hug. "Sleep on it."

"Okay." Austin smiled. He swung around and trudged out of the door and up the stairs.

The house was quiet again and he wondered where Tyler's Pack was. Normally Tyler's house was full of people, but he didn't think they were staying there that night. He wondered about it, but not enough to turn around and ask Tyler. Instead, he strolled to his closed bedroom door and paused with his hand on the knob.

When Kiley had gone upstairs, he'd assumed she would go to his room. Now he had time to think about it, Austin was pretty sure her first thought wouldn't have been the same. Damn, why hadn't he been clearer on what he wanted? Climbing into bed beside her and wrapping his arms around her slim body would have been Heaven. He doubted that would happen, so he hesitated at the threshold. He could go find out what room she was staying in, but what if she wanted to be alone?

Shaking his head, Austin turned the knob and pushed open the door.

The quiet and silence in the room didn't give him much hope. Kiley's scent was still strong, but so was the aroma of their lovemaking. The room was almost pitch-black, which was surprising since he'd left the curtains open a little the night before.

A rustle of sheets had him freezing in place. He strained to see, his sight adjusting to the dark. His shifter abilities let him easily make out a body under the blankets. Austin smiled, crossing the room to peer down at the sleeping form. Kiley lay on her stomach with one arm stretched out on to the side, while the other was hidden under a pillow. He placed a soft kiss against the nape of her neck, breathing in her clean, fresh scent. Kiley didn't even move.

He needed a shower before he joined her. She'd obviously bathed and slipped under the sheets naked and while he planned to let her rest, he'd also wake her with some special attention. Austin looked over at her one last time then strode toward the bathroom. She'd hung the damp towel on the rack and he buried his face in the cotton, breathing deeply. Damn, he was turning into a desperate fool who couldn't get enough of her. There was no way he'd be able to leave her behind. He needed to come up with a plan to get her to go home with him. All he hoped for was time would show her what he already knew — that they belonged together.

* * * *

Waking, Kiley stretched. Her body brushed against Austin's and she'd closed her eyes to enjoy the feeling when he tightened his arm around her waist. She could get used to waking up with him every morning.

His hard cock nestled between her legs and she scooted back, wriggling around just a little. In his sleep, Austin groaned softly. With a wicked grin, she turned carefully in his arms prior to squirming her way down his body. Kiley began kissing his chest, then licking lower.

It was easy enough to push him onto his back, as he

remained pliant. Kiley settled between his legs before returning her attention to Austin's body. His shaft was trapped between her breasts while she ran her tongue along the muscles of his stomach. He tasted salty and sweet at the same time. Pushing her chest against his cock, Kiley dipped her tongue into his belly button.

That got a response. Austin kicked out his legs.

Moving down enough to grip his erection, Kiley itched to taste him. The first sample of pre-cum exploded in her mouth, wakening her taste buds. Holding the base of his cock with one hand, Kiley sucked and lapped at him.

Him filling her mouth as she lowered her head again and again felt so perfect.

Moisture dripped down his shaft, helping her jack him. His cock was both firm and yielding in her palm. She squeezed his flesh again and again and over, loving how much power she had over him. While she sucked him, Kiley also humped the sheets—she couldn't help it. She was wet and needy and even though she didn't want to stop pleasuring him, Kiley needed relief, too.

"Harder," Austin demanded, lifting his hips and pushing his cock deeper down her throat. He ran his fingers through her hair, then gripped her head hard when she sucked him with more strength. "Fuck!"

Yeah, that was what she wanted. Austin was always so in control, but the way he was desperately fucking her mouth showed he no longer had the restraint he normally relied on. Kiley loved it.

"I'm gonna come," he told her. "Are you gonna swallow me down?"

Hell, yeah, she was! Instead of answering, Kiley took his erection to the full extent she was able. She choked a little and backed off to repeat the move.

"Yes!" he hissed, humping into her and holding her against his pelvis.

Kiley was rewarded with his warm cum. She swallowed as much as she could, although some of the fluid leaked down her chin. When he grew soft, she lifted her head to peer down at him. Austin lurched up and covered her mouth with his. She didn't have time to brace herself before her back landed on the mattress and Austin speared her with two fingers.

"Please!" she begged, wrapping one hand around his wrist to make him give her what she needed.

Austin attacked her neck with his lips and teeth and she arched while thrusting her hips to get his fingers deeper. She shook and panted, but it still wasn't enough.

"Austin," she pleaded.

He laughed wildly, then added a third digit while biting down on her shoulder.

She might have screamed when she climaxed. The sound echoed in her head, but she had no idea how loud she'd truly been. Nor did she care.

It wasn't until she breathed easily again that Kiley noticed Austin hovering above her with a look of amazement on his face. She blinked quickly to try to clear her vision, but no, he still stared down.

"What?" she rasped.

"You are so beautiful," he told her.

"Oh!" What could she say to that?

Austin chuckled. "So beautiful." He stroked her cheek with a gentle hand.

Kiley smiled up at him. He was really the attractive one of them, but she had no motivation to correct him.

"I was planning on waking you up in a similar fashion, but you beat me to it," he told her.

Kiley nodded. "Guess you should have gotten up sooner."

He nipped her chin but smiled. "I don't know. I'm not going to complain about my wake-up call."

She enjoyed running her hands up and down him. She wasn't going to complain about her treat, so that must make them even. Austin groaned and flopped onto his back then grasped her arm to roll her over to where her body covered his.

It was a nice morning. The room was cool and quiet and Kiley did not want to have to get out of the bed. She knew that wasn't an option, though.

"I guess we have to get up," she said.

"I need to talk to you first."

Kiley lifted her head to see his face. "What's wrong?"

"Nothing." Austin shook his head. "Or it might be nothing."

Crap, the morning started off so well.

Kiley sat up slowly then pulled the comforter over her body. She didn't want to have a serious talk naked and from the look on Austin's face, this was going to pretty serious. He sighed, sitting up, too, but he put his back to the headboard and only had the sheet covering his lap. Kiley kept her gaze on his chest, not meeting his eyes.

"I need to return home," Austin said quietly.

No! she wanted to scream. It was too soon. She didn't want to let go of him yet. Instead of saying all that, though, Kiley simply nodded. She didn't trust herself not to beg him to stay. What had she thought? That Austin would give up his Pack so they could date? She'd been an idiot.

"I know you promised Tyler you'd look after Jesse, but I could use your help, as well," Austin said.

Kiley snapped up her head to look at him. "What?"

Austin reached over and grasped her hand between hers. "I want you to come home with me."

She shook her head, not letting him finish the sentence.

"See, I knew you'd say that, but I want you to hear me out," Austin said.

Even though Kiley had thought about it, and really felt as though she wouldn't ever be happy where she was, the idea of going into another Alpha's territory terrified her, even if that Alpha was Austin.

"With the new Pack members who joined us after Riker left here, it's not easy to give everyone what is necessary all the time. I'm trying to figure out how to be the Alpha they need while giving them the space and time to heal."

She nodded. It would be a delicate balance, but she believed Austin had the Pack's best interests at heart.

"Since you come from the same Pack and know what Riker was capable of, what he did to them, it might help if they could talk to you about their experiences."

"Are you kidding me?" That was a horrible idea. "They won't want to talk to me."

"Why not?" he asked, sounding honestly confused.

"Most of them didn't even know I was being kept against my will. Only my family, some of Riker's inner circle and a few of his *friends* who he brought around. The story was that I'd been sent away to school."

"But they know differently now," Austin pointed out. "I think it'll help them."

"You think it will help me." Kiley narrowed her eyes searching his expression.

He dipped his head once in acknowledgment.

"I don't need you to fix me, Austin."

"I'm not trying to," he replied quickly.

Kiley didn't believe him. It was in Austin's nature to fix things.

"But I also want you to think about this. You don't have to stay any longer than necessary, but I'm hoping you might find a reason to stay."

"You mean you?" she asked bluntly.

"Yes," he admitted. "Things between us could blossom into so much more. If you'll give them a chance."

"I'm a Rogue shifter," Kiley pointed out. "Not many Alphas would want me in their territory."

"We both know that's bullshit. You might not have a Pack, but you also don't have the same traits other Rogues do. You just haven't found where you belong."

"And you think my place is with you?"

"Honestly, yes."

He sounded so sure. How could he know that? Kiley did not have the same faith as Austin did.

"Please give me a few weeks?" Austin asked.

Why did she want to say yes? Kiley knew it wouldn't work out, no matter how much time she spent with Austin, but she wasn't ready for it to end right then. She was a hot mess and it might not be fair to Austin, but she wasn't going to walk away yet.

"What about Jesse?" she asked. Kiley would need to put her own desires to the side if Jesse would be in danger by her leaving.

"I've spoken to Tyler. It was actually Cain and Tyler who suggested you come back with me."

"Really?" Was Tyler tired of her? He'd already mentioned to her he didn't really think Kiley belonged.

"Whatever you're thinking," Austin said, "stop. Tyler cares about you, and you know it. He just wants you to be happy."

Suddenly, Kiley was exhausted. The feelings from the previous night rose and she had to hold off tears. The sadness and disappointment in realizing that no matter how much she'd fought against joining the Pack, deep down she'd wanted to, were strong. Kiley didn't know how to deal with all the conflicting emotions.

"Hey." Austin took her face. "It might do you some good to put distance between you and here. It could only help, at least."

She found herself nodding. Okay, she would do this and see where she was after. Even if she ended up heartbroken and alone, at least Kiley would be able to move on from it all. The territory, Pack life, Tyler, Jesse, Gray and Austin.

* * * *

Kiley hugged Jesse for what felt like the millionth time in the last hour. She knew she needed to let go of the little girl, but she didn't seem to be able to. She had tried so hard not to get attached to anyone, but she hadn't seen what everyone else had and so had formed bonds with them even if she wasn't sure when it had happened.

Jesse had yelled and argued when she'd found out Kiley would be leaving. The little girl had calmed down a little when Jesse learned Kiley was to stay with Austin's Pack until things had settled down. Apparently, she had spent a lot of time there visiting. Kiley had told her she'd need help learning the territory and since Jesse had been there so much, maybe she'd be able to show her around. The girl had happily agreed.

Kiley had told Austin she'd stay until she thought the Pack was safe and happy. He had only smiled at her and said she'd always be welcome. She knew he hoped she would never want to leave, but Kiley wasn't ready to make that kind of commitment. She didn't know if she ever would. Tyler's territory might be where she had been born and raised, but Kiley didn't feel any connection to the land like she should. When she shifted, her wolf remained anxious and scared, remembering the bad times. This trip was for her as much as it was for Austin's Pack. Kiley needed to know if there was anywhere she'd finally feel safe.

Home, she thought bitterly. She hadn't had one of those in so long, she'd forgotten the feeling. Although she'd enjoyed the apartment she'd rented, it didn't compare to having a house, a place that was hers, a place to be comfortable and protected. Maybe Tyler had been right and she would find where she was meant to be. But still, her chest tightened and she could feel the panic wanting to set in. She'd tried not to think about what this would mean for her and Austin, too.

Once again Austin gave her the time she needed to figure things out on her own, but she knew he hoped she wanted a real relationship with him. The reason why her head was spinning. Without the few people around she actually considered her friends, Kiley was going to face this new challenge all on her own.

Gray and Dominic stepped out of the front door and joined her and Jesse on the steps. Kiley released Jesse and urged the young girl to her uncle. It hurt to leave all of them, because she did wonder if she'd ever make it back. There was a reason she hadn't left. She hadn't wanted Riker's actions to keep her from her birthplace, but Kiley had also feared if she'd ever left she'd never return. Now she was testing that theory.

"We'll miss you," Dominic told her in his deep, relaxing voice. He didn't speak a lot, except to Jesse, but when he did, it was a pleasure to listen to the cadence of his voice.

"I'll miss you all, too," she admitted softly. She had to fight the urge to get teary-eyed.

"You'll always be welcome, Kiley. Don't forget that," Dominic told her and bent for Jesse. "One last hug. Austin's on his way out."

The two females hugged each other. Finally, Kiley pulled away and placed Jesse in his arms. "I love you, little cub," she whispered to the girl.

She spun away quickly as she heard Dominic and Jesse leave. She wiped at the tears that had fallen.

"Kiley." Gray said her name softly.

She dropped her head—this was going to be equally as difficult. She took a deep breath and turned to him. The emotion in his eyes surprised her. They had spent a lot of time together and cared deeply for each other. Her heart broke a little at the look of loss on his face.

"Oh, Gray," she murmured, cupping his cheek. "I'm so sorry. I have been terrible to you."

He shook his head but she wouldn't let him argue. She hadn't once stopped to think about how her feelings for Austin would affect Gray. She hadn't been able to give to Gray even the little she already felt for Austin.

"I am so sorry, Gray. I didn't think—"

"Shh," he told her, pulling her into his arms. "It's okay. I'm going to miss you like crazy, but we both knew this would be happening one day. Eventually one of us was going to find the person we were truly meant to be with."

Kiley laughed nervously. "I wouldn't go that far."

His chuckle sounded warm and she hoped she'd hear it again. She wasn't leaving for some unknown country without phones, for God's sake. She could talk to her friends, to Jesse and keep tabs on the Pack.

"Give him a chance," Gray urged. "He makes such a good match for you."

"Yeah." She blushed a little while shifting from foot to foot. "I don't know."

"Please, for me."

Well, damn, Gray never asked anything from her. Kiley wrapped her arms around his waist and hugged him tightly. "I'll always love you," she vowed sincerely.

"I know." He embraced her in turn. "I'll always wish I was your mate."

A tear slipped down her cheek. "You'll find her," she promised. "And I hope she's ten times as stubborn as you say I am."

He laughed like she'd intended. "Me too."

With two fingers under her chin, he placed a soft kiss on her lips. There was nothing sexual about it—it was a goodbye to how they'd once been.

They smiled into each other's eyes. That was how Tyler and Austin found them.

Kiley was pleased by Austin's reaction. While almost every other wolf she knew would have felt threatened and attacked, Austin didn't. He walked calmly down the steps. Gray dropped his hand from her face, and when Austin offered his, the two men shook.

"Best of luck in getting answers. If there is anything at all you need, give me a call," Austin told him. "And try to keep your Alpha out of trouble. You know how he is."

Gray nodded. "Thank you, Austin. I'll do my best."

Austin faced Tyler then pulled him into a hug. "I'll talk to you soon."

"Be careful driving," Tyler advised Austin before addressing Kiley. "We'll talk soon."

"I…I'll miss you," Kiley managed. There was so much she wanted to say, but the words wouldn't come.

"Come hug me." Tyler opened his arms and she jumped

into them. Even though Tyler was close to her own age, the embrace felt like that of a father. She closed her eyes and breathed him in so she would have his scent with her.

Tyler held her close for several moments and even kissed the top of her head. Kiley rubbed her cheek against his chest. She'd never touched him like that before, but it made her feel protected. She managed to break away and, without looking at anyone, walked to her SUV. Austin said something else behind her, then rushed up to catch her. He threw his arm around her neck as he escorted her across the drive. When he stopped at a black Explorer and opened the passenger door, she looked up at him blankly.

"Come on," he urged. "Climb in—we need to get on the road."

She'd started to follow his instruction before her brain connected. She stepped back. "What about my car?" Kiley hadn't even thought about her ride.

"Tyler will take care of it." He pressed his hand on the small of her back, trying to get her to move. "Gray already agreed to keep an eye on your apartment, too."

"But I need it," she argued, her feet firmly planted.

"Kiley," Austin said, sounding tired. "Get in. We will get you another vehicle if you want. You can have this one. Or someone else can drive yours. I don't care."

"We should have discussed this better. I just assumed I'd be driving myself. I need a way to get around," she tried to explain. "And a way to get home." She wasn't trying to be difficult.

"You can drive anything you want at home," he countered. "This will be yours."

She hesitated. She didn't have much. Even her apartment had come furnished. Some clothes, pictures and knick-knacks, her computer and odds and ends. Her biggest possession was the new Tahoe. "I want to take my ride."

"Fine," Austin agreed without pause. "One of the men will drive it."

"That's silly. I can follow behind you," she offered.

"No," he dismissed. "Now, hop up."

"*No?*" Kiley repeated.

Austin's grip on the door tightened. "Don't make this an issue," he said in a voice so low he might have been talking to himself. "We need to talk about the Pack on the road. Plus…I really want to make this road trip with you."

"Oh." Kiley didn't know how to respond to that. It was very sweet and, honestly, she'd like to ride along with him. She had to have to her own vehicle. "Are you sure it won't be a big deal for one of your guys to drive it?"

Austin gently grabbed a handful of hair and pulled her forward. It didn't hurt but it surprised her. That was a move he hadn't used before…and she kind of liked it. It made her hot when he showed his strength but didn't hurt her.

"It'll probably work out better, actually. Since I want to be alone with you, two vehicles following will be safer, plus, the men will have more room for the long drive."

Kiley pressed her lips together. Well, when he put it that way… "Cool." She climbed in, refusing his help. Kiley retained her stubborn ways and she didn't want to spoil Austin into thinking she'd be giving in to all his demands.

Austin closed her door and went to the driver's side. He jumped in and locked the doors. "Put your seatbelt on," he ordered.

She laughed — he couldn't help but use the Alpha tone. Kiley did so with a smirk.

"I know you're only playing along," Austin said. "And oddly enough, I'm okay with that."

Kiley shifted in her seat to get more comfortable. She'd decided to wear a pair of soft cotton gray pants along with a light pink long-sleeved T-shirt. The athletic shoes she'd picked were her most comfortable. Her entire outfit had been chosen to make the hours ahead of her relaxing. The time she'd spent with Austin had either been under threat or high emotions, including passion. This would be the first time they'd have the opportunity to get to know each other better.

As Austin backed out of the drive, Kiley placed her hand on the window as a goodbye to those standing on the porch. She wasn't leaving forever, so why did it feel that way?

Once Austin put the vehicle in gear, she faced the front and looked ahead. "So tell me something," she requested. Kiley needed the few minutes it would take him to drive them off the Pack's land to be filled with noise. She didn't want to think anymore.

A glanced in the rear-view mirror showed her the two vehicles following them. Right behind them was Kiley's SUV and behind that Austin's black truck. There didn't seem to be anyone else driving down the two-lane road. She actually jumped when Austin covered her hand with his. She laced his fingers through his and held on to the comfort he offered.

"What do you want to talk about?" he asked.

"Anything," she replied quickly. "Something happy."

"I'm pretty sure Colt is in love with Tony," he said.

He wasn't betraying any confidences with his topic. Tony's display in front of his father, brother, Tyler and them had pretty much busted Tony and Colt's relationship right out into the open. Kiley giggled. "I'd sort of figured that out for myself."

"No, I mean this is it for him. He's is absolutely one hundred percent in love with Tony and I think Tony feels the same way," Austin shared.

"That...that's really awesome," Kiley commented. She'd seen the attraction between Tony and Colt but hadn't known they were as close as she'd found out. "Tony is going to need someone strong at his side during the next phase of going public."

"That's exactly what I was thinking. I think I'm going to be losing my Beta and best friend."

"Oh." Kiley squeezed his fingers. "Sorry."

"I'm happy for him, even if it makes me a little sad. But if anyone can support Tony the way he's going to need, it will be Colt."

"It's kinda cool, though," she said.

"Yeah," he chuckled. "It is."

They were driving past the county line and she resisted looking behind her. She'd be back. Three or four weeks and Kiley would return to her lonely apartment, taking pictures of cheating spouses and picking up men at bars. It wouldn't ever have the intensity or rightness she felt with Austin, but it would be safer. Or maybe she would go somewhere else altogether.

"I thought you wanted me to distract you," Austin said quietly.

"I did...do," she told him. Kiley hadn't expected to get jealous over the conversation. Tony and Colt would find a way to be together despite Tony's huge responsibility and still Kiley believed they'd end up happy.

Kiley wasn't that lucky. Austin sat next to her and still she wasn't able to see a future where the two of them would be able to last. She had a real chance of finding what everyone else wanted and longed for, but instead of embracing Austin, she was making plans to leave him.

What in the hell was she doing? Tyler had urged her to try to see where things could lead with Austin and Kiley was doing the opposite. Instead of going around and around with her feelings, Kiley had a decision to make. She'd made harder choices and never with the results she'd be after this time. In the end, she might be happy with Austin—she knew it was possible. Kiley just needed to be brave enough to take the chance.

Here and now she vowed to at least follow the path laid out in front of her.

"Hey, you okay?" he asked gently.

"Yeah." Kiley smiled. "I think I am." She released his hand and stroked up his leg, lingering on the zipper of his jeans.

"What are you doing?"

"Nothing," she said innocently.

"Kiley." His word almost a growl.

"What, hon?" she teased. With her nail, she scraped the outside of his pants along his cock. Austin rolled his shoulders and shifted in his seat. "You okay?"

"You know damn well what you're doing to me right now," he accused.

She laughed. "And what would I be doing?"

Again, she faintly brushed over his erection. Austin grabbed her hand and pressed it fully against his dick.

"Keep that up, baby, and I will pull this car over."

She closed fingers over him. Now they were getting somewhere. That was exactly what she wanted. "That would be a shame."

"Since we have two vehicles full of guards behind us, yes, it would be."

She stiffened and looked behind her. Well, shit, he had a damn good point there.

Austin chuckled. "Forgot about them, didn't you?"

"I seem to forget everything when I'm close to you," she muttered under her breath.

"Me, too," he told her. "But I don't think that's necessarily a bad thing."

Neither did she. Kiley placed her palm on his knees before laying her head on his seat, close enough to pick up his masculine scent. She closed her eyes and relaxed, to enjoy his presence.

Chapter Seven

The drive seemed to take forever, yet at the same time, it ended way too soon. Once Austin told her they were just outside their territory, her stomach jumped around. She and Austin did a lot of talking as they traveled closer to Austin's territory. There had been moments where they'd simply sat quietly, but the silence had always been comfortable. She'd learned about Austin's dreams and his hopes for his Pack. During that time, she'd fallen more than a little bit in love with him.

Austin cared about those he'd been charged to protect. Actually, it was more than that—he loved his Pack. Each and every member. This Kiley knew.

While the scenery that passed outside the window was indeed beautiful, it didn't take the edge off. Green grass, tall healthy trees and plenty of open space flew by them. Kiley clenched her hands in her lap to keep herself from telling Austin to turn around. She jumped when Austin's palm covered her fist.

"Relax." They reached a dirt track and Austin pulled onto it. "Almost there."

Kiley continued to stare out of the window as they bumped along the road. She was trying to see the Alpha house and gates. About a mile from where they'd turned off, a large cabin came into view. She glanced at Austin, but he merely smiled. Kiley took in the home they pulled up in front of. It was the most beautiful place she had ever seen. Dark, thick wooden logs made up the outside. It boasted a wide wraparound porch and huge windows that would look out onto the woods mere feet away. If she'd picked any house, it would have been one very similar to this.

Austin put the vehicle in park and switched off the engine. "Well, this is it."

Kiley glanced over at him, confused. "This? This is your house?"

"Yes," he said with a frown. "You don't like it?"

Kiley quickly unfastened her seat belt and pushed open the door before rushing forward. The large cabin stood, warm and inviting. Austin stepped up behind her and placed his hand on the small of her back. She closed the distance, leaning her body against his.

"So, you like it then?" he asked with uncertainty in his voice.

Kiley nodded. "I think it's wonderful." She really was in awe of the place. The cabin had been built out in the middle of nowhere, in perfect seclusion, with the woods so close she smelled them. The trees, the animals who lived inside, a source of water...

Her wolf rippled inside her. Yes, she wanted to run. But there would be time for that.

"Let me show you the inside," Austin said, leading her forward.

The steps were solid and when she reached the front porch she saw several wicker chairs and even a swing.

"You sit out here a lot?" she asked, hoping he did. She would love to spend time sitting with him.

"I do," Austin answered. "I like relaxing out here at night. When everything has slowed down and I can take the time to listen to nature. Plus, it helps me bond with the territory and Pack."

They turned as he spoke and looked out from the porch. Wide-openness filled Kiley's vision and she felt comforted by it.

"You don't have any gates?" She had never in her life lived within a territory that didn't have security gates. Even Tyler's home had them.

"The Pack is so small I have never seen the need for

them. I didn't want any of the members to feel they are not welcome in my home. We stay hidden from everyone else and haven't had any problems with other Packs. We only want to live peacefully. That may change with everything that's happening, but for now, I like the simplicity of living here."

"That's perfect," Kiley said with a sigh. She hadn't meant to say that out loud but once the words had slipped through, she wasn't sorry. Austin had a territory to be proud of. It wouldn't hurt to let him know she thought he was a great Alpha.

Quietly, they made their way to the front door. Austin withdrew his key and inserted it into the lock but paused to look over at her. "I want you to think of this as your home, too, Kiley. You know I'm hoping you find a place here."

She opened her mouth to reply, but he held up a hand.

"I'm not pushing you, but while you're here, I want you to at least try."

"I'm going to," she assured him. "Not only for you or your Pack, but for myself. I hope I can find a home here, too. Where I'll be happy."

His smile lit up his entire face and made his gaze appear softer.

"It's just me and Colt here and we're pretty easy. If you want to change anything, then change it. If you wish to add something, then add it."

She was a pretty casual girl herself and she couldn't imagine making changes to the house, but she did wonder what the cabin of two bachelors would look like on the inside.

Austin unlocked the door and pushed it open. Kiley stepped in first and her breath caught in her throat. The front door opened to a large open area. The same dark wood used outside lined the cabin's walls and ceilings. Steps led into a room with large black leather couches and chairs, a big-screen TV and a monster stereo system. Kiley grinned and walked down the steps into the room. She looked over it with a critical eye.

The stone fireplace in the corner looked amazing. A couple of pictures of wolves hung on the wall and thick rugs graced the floor throughout the room. She turned and looked into the kitchen. Oh, that room was even better! Even though she wasn't much of a cook, something obvious from the barbecue disaster at Tyler's, she still appreciated a kitchen like the one Austin had.

"Oh, wow!" she finally said.

Austin chuckled and swung his arm around her shoulders. "I take it you approve."

"Yes," she told him turning. "You have a lovely home."

"We. *We* have a lovely home," he corrected. "Hopefully."

Kiley stretched onto her tiptoes. "I'm glad I came."

Austin closed the distance and covered her lips with his. Kiley gripped his shoulders hard, losing all sense of direction and letting her mind drift away. The only thing she concentrated on was the feel of him against her

"First things first," he said against her mouth.

Kiley wasn't sure what he meant until Austin lowered her down so her back met the leather couch. His tongue worked magic and she arched up when he pressed his hand over her cotton-covered pussy.

"Austin." She panted out his name when he took his mouth from hers.

"Gotta have you," he said desperately. "Gotta have you now! I can't believe you're here. That we're here together."

They hurriedly removed her clothes as he nibbled and licked her neck. Kiley tilted her head to the side to give him better access. It felt so good and he made her tremble.

"God! I burn for you," he confessed.

The zipper of his jeans came down. Kiley used her feet to help push the fabric down his thighs. He lined his cock up with her entrance and she marveled at the solid heat of him entering her.

He slid in slowly and easily now she was used to his body. Once fully seated, he paused and Kiley met his gaze. Kiley ran her fingers along his cheek and drew him down to her.

"Kiss me," she whispered against his lips.

He closed his eyes and took a deep breath before slamming his mouth on hers. They kissed and he started to move inside her, each stroke slow and deep. Kiley ran her hands over his lower back, urging him on. Austin made love to her slowly. They'd never touched or caressed so gently. Eyes locked together, each breath shared, their bodies moved in rhythm. It was the single best experience of her life. When she fell over the edge, she cried out his name, tightening around him.

Her beating heart pounded while Kiley wrapped her arms around Austin and held on as she calmed. His thrusts were erratic, but he still softly held her. Austin shuddered above her, his face buried in her neck. It was too good a moment to let go. She was sad when he found completion and came.

Her ears were still ringing when she heard the slamming of a car door. The moment broke and Kiley froze. Austin jumped up.

"Who…?" she started to ask, but he shook his head with a smile on his face.

"Hope you're ready, baby," he told her, gathering her clothes and placing them in her arms. "Looks as though you're about to meet the other woman in my life."

Confused and more than a little upset by his declaration, Kiley hurriedly dressed, copying Austin. She'd just finished when the front door burst open.

"Austin! Colt! Are you home?" a woman called out.

She closed the door and stopped. With the open rooms, she got a look at Kiley as Kiley got a look at her. She was a smaller woman with short brown hair. She wore jeans and a T-shirt that said, *'Yes, I am a princess'*. She was around Kiley's age and obviously felt right at home walking down the steps.

"Who are you?" she demanded.

Kiley frowned. "Who are you?" she retorted, crossing her arms over her chest. If this was a girlfriend or special member of the Pack, Kiley didn't want to make an enemy, even though her heart ached with betrayal. Why would Austin want her there if he already had someone else?

"Girls," Austin drawled, and they both turned to him.

"What's going on?" the other woman questioned.

He motioned her forward. She smiled and walked directly into his arms. Kiley didn't even try to tamp down the growl that escaped her throat. She did, however, resist ripping the woman to shreds — barely. *Great.* Austin was going to know how much she truly cared for him. He'd made a fool of her.

"Ginger! Ginger," he said lovingly. "I want you to meet someone. This is Kiley Palmer."

"Kiley?" Ginger exclaimed loudly. "The chick from the bar?"

Austin nodded. "Yes, the one I told you about." He waved his hand, gesturing for Kiley to go to him. "Kiley, this is my sister, Ginger," he introduced.

"Your *sister*?" Kiley snapped. *What the fuck?* She'd had no idea Austin had a sister. She was even more surprised when the other woman smacked Austin in the back of the head.

"Ow! Shit! What was that for?" he complained, rubbing his hand over the spot.

"She thought I was your lover, you dumbass," Ginger enlightened him.

Austin's eyes widened and he rushed over to her. "Oh, no, crap, damn."

Kiley let Austin wrap his arms around her, watching the other woman watch her.

Ginger grinned and rocked on the heels of her feet. "I can't believe you found her."

Kiley caught Austin's blush. "What?"

"I might have returned to the bar, searched the web, you know…a few things," he confessed.

She laughed. "Oh, my God! You were stalking me!"

"I was not." He sounded indigent.

"He totally was," Ginger said with a smile. "And I think

we're going to get along famously."

Kiley grinned back at her. "Yeah, me, too."

"There's got to be a story here," Ginger said. "Would you like a cup of coffee or something?"

Kiley groaned. "I'd love some coffee. I had a long drive."

"Great." Ginger put her arm through Kiley's and pulled. "While I make a pot, you can tell me all about how you and Austin hooked up again."

"Sure," she agreed. She allowed Austin's sister to drag her into the beautiful kitchen, but not before sending Austin an amused look over her shoulder. It appeared Austin had left out the most colorful part of his life. She would pay him back for that. Kiley could think of a dozen fun and erotic ways to get her revenge.

The spacious kitchen gleamed clean and warm. She sat at one of the bar stools against the marble island. Ginger went directly to the freezer and pulled out a bag of coffee.

"So, spill," Ginger told her.

"So, there I was working a job and Gray Mason comes to summon me to Tyler's house…"

* * * *

Austin ducked out of the kitchen into the living room with a smile at the ringing of his cell phone. After the initial shock and misunderstanding, Kiley and Ginger had become fast friends, just like he'd thought. He hadn't told Kiley about his sister because Ginger wasn't always easy to handle. But she was the sweetest and most loyal woman he knew.

Colt's number flashed over the caller ID. "Hey, man," Austin greeted.

"Hi, did you get home?" Colt asked.

"Safe and sound. Ginger is here and the ladies are ganging up on me." Why that made him so happy, he was not about to admit over the phone.

"Good. Do me a favor and stay close by the guards."

Austin's stomach dropped. "What happened?"

"The guy's still not talking much, but he did say one thing."

"What?" Austin asked cautiously.

Colt hesitated. "Prepare for war."

"So, someone else might be after us." He'd really hoped this was all about someone trying to intimidate Tony and now they'd found the three shifters, everyone was safe.

"I believe so. Since we didn't agree to go public, maybe they will leave us alone — if you want to take the chance?" Colt asked.

"No," Austin stated firmly. "I won't put the Pack in danger by ignoring any threat. Plus, our friends will need all the help they can get."

"I think so. Tony finally spoke to the Prince of Felines. He's agreed to meet with us. He said he didn't know anything about the threat but he wasn't surprised," Colt informed him.

"I didn't even know they had a Prince until this happened."

"I guess they have a royal family. Not that they have much control over the shifters. But the Prince seemed upset about it and we're going to meet with him when we get to Grand Falls."

"That's the shifter who's mated to the vampire and the witch, right?" Austin had heard a while back about the Alpha taking unusual mates.

Colorado was broken into three territories. His, Tyler's and Tom's. While his Pack was small, and Tyler's consisted only of wolf shifters, Tom actually had several different animal shifters in his area. Plus vampires and other paranormal creatures.

"Yeah," Colt said, amused. "Gotta tell you, I'm curious about how an Alpha can handle those relationships."

Austin agreed. He couldn't imagine having to add a Master vampire to the relationship.

"Call me when you head out. I'll call Tom later and speak to him."

"Will do," Colt agreed.

"Okay. Talk to you soon."

Austin hung up and stared out of the large window to the territory surrounding the house. He'd always loved being out in the open and the freedom it provided. Now he worried that by not having the same security as other Alphas, he was making it easier for an attack to happen. Before he thought too much about it, his name was called from the kitchen. He joined Kiley and his sister, the two women giggling about something.

Ginger stood in front of the stove, stirring a saucepan, while Kiley sat on top of the counter watching. He strolled over to her, trying to convey everything was okay. But when he kissed her cheek, she must have noticed something off about him because she frowned.

"What's wrong?" she asked.

Austin shook his head and offered her a smile. "Nothing, got a lot on my mind."

She pressed her lips together but didn't call him on his lie. It was obvious Kiley didn't believe him.

"I've got some phone calls to make. There may be some members of the Pack stopping by in the morning," he told her, trying to sound casual.

"Austin." She grabbed his arm when he tried to move away. "Tell me what's going on."

He knew he really didn't have the option of not telling her. "We have trouble with the feline shifters." He watched a series of emotions cross her face until she got control.

"Whatever it is, we'll handle it." She tried to smile. "That is what you brought me here for."

It wasn't the only reason and they both knew it. But he'd promised to give her time and he was a man of his word. Austin cupped her face and made sure their eyes locked. "We will."

They stared at each other until Ginger broke the tension. "I still can't believe everything you all have been through," Ginger said.

"Yeah, it's crazy," Austin agreed. "Let me know when the food's ready?"

Kiley nodded as Ginger waved him off. "Leave. That way I can get the gossip about Colt out of Kiley."

Laughing, he let the two most important women in his life talk while he made his way to the spare room he'd remade into his office. He pushed open the door, pleased to see all his belongings were still in the right places. A couple who ran a cleaning service took care of his house for him and it seemed Elizabeth and Roman hadn't forgotten him. Not that he'd expected them to.

Austin pulled his keys out of his pocket then unlocked his filing cabinet before doing the same to the desk drawers. He trusted his Pack, but since several members confided in him, Austin always made sure he kept everything that had to do with his Pack locked up. He would never betray the information entrusted to him. It wasn't easy to keep tabs on everyone as it used to be with his Pack growing. And now, with Colt gone, he needed extra help. Kiley was who he wanted by his side, but she wasn't ready quite yet. Hopefully one day they'd mate and the Pack would be able to go to her for things he was currently solely responsible for.

He didn't believe it was only wishful thinking anymore, either.

Their lovemaking had been more intimate than previous times. Kiley might not be able to say the words yet, but he'd seen in her eyes that she felt something very strong for him. They were meant to be together and time would show her.

Austin pulled out his phone list and opened it up. He needed more guards on duty and a meeting with his inner circle first thing in the morning.

Austin was still on the phone when dinner was ready so Ginger put his plate in the oven to stay warm. Apparently that was a normal occurrence, but Kiley didn't like it. Sure, he was a busy man, but in order to take care of his Pack, he needed to take care of himself first.

She didn't say anything, but Kiley planned to bring up her thoughts with Austin. If he truly wanted her there to help the Pack, then Austin was going to have to listen to her.

After she and Ginger finished, Kiley rinsed off the plates and placed them in the dishwasher. She might not be a chef, but she could clean up after a good meal. And Ginger had cooked a chicken pasta dish that had been marvelous.

"So." Ginger looked around the kitchen. "Want to see the outside?"

Kiley shrugged. She wasn't tired yet and Austin was still holed up in his office. "Sure."

The back door was in the living room beside the full window. Kiley followed behind Ginger and when she stepped outside, she grinned. The sun was starting to set, the orange and red colors fading in the distance. Green grass and trees stretched far and wide. "I love it here," she said out loud, not really talking to Ginger.

"Yeah," Ginger agreed.

They stood in silence, lost in their own thoughts, for several minutes before Ginger stirred and walked to the right.

"Over there." She pointed to the east set of trees. "There's a small trail that leads deeper into the wildness. That is where the majority of the Pack live. Some members live in town but most of us prefer the openness here."

Looking closely, Kiley saw the narrow trail Ginger had been talking about. It was obviously made to remain hidden unless a person knew to look for it.

"Wow!" Kiley exclaimed in appreciation. "That's nice."

"When we left our birth Pack, Austin promised we would always have open space. We traveled from Minnesota until we found this place. Austin said he felt the pull of home and we searched and searched until we came here."

"This isn't your birth Pack?" Kiley asked.

"Just what have you and my brother been doing if you

didn't know that?" Ginger inquired with a lifted eyebrow and a smirk.

Kiley blushed. It seemed that with learning each other's bodies, and worrying, they really hadn't spent a lot of time talking. "Well, you know," Kiley tried to explain with a wave of her hand.

Ginger giggled like a little girl. "Yeah, I think I got it."

Kiley ignored the woman's obvious amusement. "It's complicated."

"I'm sure it is," Ginger agreed too easily then grew serious. "This, all of this space and the people and everything that comes with being an Alpha, Austin deserves. He's a great Alpha."

Kiley didn't respond but simply stared out as the sun dipped lower and lower on the horizon. "I think he is."

"I'm glad you came." Ginger turned toward her. "Our Pack was really small before we started to take in Riker's people. Austin cares for everyone and he needs help. We want to offer comfort, of course, but we don't know what they've been through."

Kiley knew too well what her Pack mates had suffered. "Yeah, I doubt most want to talk about it."

"That's the thing," Ginger said. "Some do. I just don't know what to say to them. Austin tries and they seem comfortable with him, but he only has so many hours in the day and there's still other Pack business to take care of."

"I know," Kiley agreed. Austin had told her the exact same thing when he'd asked her to come back with him. "I'm going to do my best to show them someone cares and that they're safe."

"It's going to be great." Austin stepped out onto the back porch with them, smiling. "I've already spoken to the inner circle and they are excited. I also called a few of the new members who came from Riker's Pack and told them and they all want to see you."

Kiley faced him and almost choked. He'd been running his hands through his hair, making the strands stick up at odd angles. Austin had pushed up the sleeves on his sweater, showing off his toned forearms, and her mouth literally watered. She wanted him, craved his touch. She must have made a sound, or he'd seen what she was thinking about on her face, because he strode over to her and, ignoring his sister's smirk, leaned down and took Kiley's mouth in a deep, sensual kiss.

Damn, she would never tire of the taste of him. Kiley moaned and wrapped an arm around his neck, holding him close. Austin went down on his knees and yanked her to the edge of her chair. Their tongues tangled and dueled for control, before she gave in and tilted her head to allow him the lead.

"Well, I think I'm headed home," Ginger stated loudly.

Austin pulled his mouth away from Kiley's but remained embracing her tightly. "Make sure you're careful. Kiley told you about the threats?" he asked his sister.

At Ginger's nod, Austin winked. "I know you can take care of yourself, but if someone is around, I would like to question them instead of just burying the body."

Kiley didn't know if he was joking or not, but having gotten to know Ginger, she highly doubted it.

"I'll be careful. Don't forget to eat. You're going to need your strength," Ginger said, laughing.

Austin groaned while Kiley didn't hold in her giggle. "Go home," he begged.

Ginger waved her hand in the air. "I'm going. I'm going."

Instead of walking into the house, Ginger leapt over the porch railing to land gracefully on her feet.

"Show-off," Austin called.

They had a strong relationship was and Kiley hoped if she stayed, they'd allow her in with the teasing and jokes. She'd never had that kind of easiness with anyone.

Once his sister was far enough away enough to be out of hearing distance, Austin held Kiley's face, searching. "You okay?" he asked

She nodded. "Better than I expected, actually."

"Really?" he asked. "That intrigues me."

"I've been holding back with you," she admitted. "Even though I keep saying I'll give us a try while I'm here, I find myself making alternative plans. Or at least I had been."

"Up until?" he questioned.

"I walked into your house."

"Only that?"

"Yes," she said. "I feel safe here."

Austin dipped his head. "That's what I wanted. What I hoped for." He picked her up swiftly out of the chair and sat down with her on his lap. "I imagined trying to get you comfortable in every room."

"Comfortable?" she asked, wiggling on his lap.

Austin groaned and held her still, his erection pressing into her ass. "Can't get any more comfortable in a room than being naked and screaming."

Kiley laughed, shook her head and laughed again. Her body quaked as he pulled her against his chest. When she finally stopped laughing, she wiped her eyes and twisted around to see him. "I can't argue with you there, I guess."

Austin tilted his head and faked seriousness. "So, where should we start?"

She lifted a shoulder in a shrug. "I haven't seen the bedroom yet."

"You haven't seen any of the upstairs."

She crinkled her nose and tried to be serious. "What do you plan to do about it?" she questioned.

Austin rose with her still in his arms. She grunted and protested when he slung her over his shoulder.

"Austin, put me down!"

He ignored her in favor of making his way to the side door. Austin locked it behind them while starting the tour. "Okay, so this is the living room, which you should already be comfortable in."

She kicked her feet and he had to tighten his grip. "Yes, the living room. I got that."

Austin slapped her ass once and she gasped. "I'm giving

you the grand tour. Work with me."

"I would work with you better if everything was not upside down," she complained.

Austin chuckled and slapped her ass again. She wiggled around, enjoying the heat that spread.

"Okay, over there is the laundry room." He waved his hand in its general direction. "You saw the kitchen…over there is my office. There's a study next to it, but if you want to use it for your office or anything else, that would work too." He reached the stairs. "That door leads to the bathroom down here. Usually only guests use it." He started up. "Now, up here is the really good stuff."

"Austin, come on, put me down. All the blood's rushing to my head," Kiley pleaded. She had to at least act as though she was protesting, even though she was quite enjoying the ride.

"So, there are four bedrooms up here. Two guest, Colt's, and my room. Ginger has stuff stashed in one of them, but the other is free for any visitors. You can sleep there, but I'm really hoping you'll spend most of your time in here." Austin pushed his bedroom door open, brought Kiley off his shoulder and placed her on her feet in the doorway.

"Nice," she commented and walked in. He had a California King bed with a dark wood headboard and matching end tables. Off to one side was a double balcony door. The curtains were closed now, but on clear nights Austin would be able to leave the doors open when lying down. She looked forward to sharing the experience with him.

Kiley came to a stop in front of the mattress. "My, my, what a big bed you have," she teased.

He took a few steps forward and pulled his shirt over his head. "All the better to throw you on."

Kiley smirked, yanking off her shirt and dropping it to the ground. Austin paused long enough to open his pants and push them down.

"Oh, goodness. What a big cock you have." Kiley faked

shock.

Austin stroked his already fully aroused member. "All the better to fuck you with, my dear."

Kiley threw back her head, laughing hard. "Well, in that case..." she stated, before stripping the rest of her clothes off and climbing into the middle of the bed. "Get over here, my big, bad wolf."

"Woof, woof," Austin barked and pounced. He landed on the soft mattress, bouncing both of them, and grasped her around the waist to hold her close.

Kiley reached for him, giggling. Their lips connected. When they pulled away, they were both panting for breath. "I can't get enough of you," she confessed in a desperate tone. "I ache to have you inside." She wrapped her hand around his cock and stroked him, causing Austin to buck and groan. Kiley kept stroking until he grasped her wrist.

"Enough," he growled.

"Please, Austin," she begged.

Austin gripped the base of his shaft and scooted between her legs. "What, no foreplay?" he teased, running the tip between her folds.

"Fuck foreplay," she mumbled, lifting her legs off the bed and fitting them under his arms.

"You sure?"

Kiley narrowed her eyes. She wasn't messing around with him. "Now!"

He plunged in, not pausing until he was buried deep.

Kiley arched and dropped her head onto the pillow. "Yes, yes."

"Gonna be fast. Down and dirty," he warned, lifting her hips and bracing his knees.

Kiley opened her eyes and met his gaze. "Do it."

In a blink of an eye, Austin withdrew his cock before flipping her over onto her stomach. "Hang on to the headboard," he ordered.

She climbed onto her knees then lowered her chest to the mattress while wrapping her hands around the wood.

Austin palmed her ass as he left a trail of pre-cum against her leg. The heat was swamping her so Kiley pushed back, hoping he would get the message.

"Austin—"

Kiley didn't get to finish her sentence. Austin thrust deep and her breath whooshed from her. He grabbed hold of her shoulders while rocking in and out of her. Damn, damn, damn, it felt so fucking good to be ridden this way. His cock slid through her wet folds and so deep her pussy was already clenching, trying to hold him inside.

Sweat dripped onto her skin but she didn't care. Each time he plunged forward, she threw herself back. It *was* down and dirty and wonderful.

"Harder," he demanded.

Kiley released one hand and brought it down to her clit. She circled the tiny nub before rubbing relentlessly.

Austin continued slamming his cock powerfully and fast and she let go. Throwing back her head, she screamed out her climax. He didn't stop. Austin pumped and pumped.

"Not done, almost, take me…take me."

"Yes," she hissed. Kiley bore down, engulfing his dick when he drove forward.

He tightened his hands on her hips when he finally howled out his release.

They collapsed on the bed in a tangle of limbs. Yes, she saw the benefit of sharing his room instead of sleeping in one of the guest beds.

"I'm never getting up again," she panted out.

"Okay." He patted her ass weakly. "Okay."

Chapter Eight

Kiley closed the door quietly behind her before tiptoeing through the house until she reached the spacious kitchen. God, she loved that room. It made her want to find some old recipe books and learn to cook the way she saw on old television shows and movies. She might have no skills in the kitchen, but Kiley made one awesome cup of coffee, so she'd have to start there.

She'd watched Ginger the previous day, so she knew where everything lived. Within a few minutes, she had a pot brewing and stood peering out of the small kitchen window over the sink. It really was a beautiful territory. So different from the one she'd grown up in.

In the distance, the mountain peaks were visible and appeared much closer than they really were. The snow-tipped tops looked appealing even though she had no interest in ever being around the cold. She hated being cold. But if she had the chance to investigate this little piece of heaven Austin had found, she would. Everything shone so brightly there. The green grass and the blue of the sky. No skyscrapers or buildings crammed all together. Here, it seemed the population was spread out and no one would intrude.

Did that mean they were safe, though?

There were no gates or barriers to keep anyone away from Austin or his Pack. Kiley had hated the compound and all the security, but what if that was the only way to live? Even though Austin wasn't planning on his Pack becoming public, what if they were exposed?

So many questions.

If she was to keep her old Pack mates safe, Kiley needed to know more. Get mixed up with Austin's business. She didn't think he'd mind. But that would put her dangerously close to the Pack and getting overly involved in their lives.

Maybe that was what she needed to do, though. She'd already promised herself she'd try with Austin, at least *attempt* a real relationship, so why not vow to do everything possible for the Pack, no matter the consequences?

The coffee pot gurgled, pulling her out of her thoughts. She made herself a mug to carry to the deck. Kiley slid open the glass then stepped out into the cool early morning air.

Dew still glistened on the porch railing and along the flowers in the beds. The aroma of freshness and foliage smelled sweet. Would she be able to pick up fragrance for miles with the openness of the territory? Kiley was tempted to shift and see, but since she didn't know the area well, she'd have to wait.

She pattered down the wood steps that led from the deck. Even though she enjoyed Austin's company, Kiley was glad to get these few minutes to herself. There was something about being in nature alone early in the morning that made her feel calm and relaxed. It'd been so long since she'd felt this peace she wanted to enjoy every minute of it.

Kiley plopped down in the middle of the grass, ignoring the dampness seeping into her pajama bottoms. Her coffee sloshed over, but she righted her cup before she spilled much. Licking the rim of her mug, Kiley hummed in appreciation of the strong brew. She loved a good cup of coffee and it appeared Austin bought the best.

"Okay," she murmured to herself, closing her eyes. "Try to connect." It might not work. There was a chance she wouldn't be able to bond to any territory again, but she needed to know.

Clearing her mind, Kiley hummed, using her enhanced senses to map the area around her. Quiet shuffling came from small animals heading that way from the north, a family of wild rabbits looking for food. The screech of a hawk high above her scouting for prey was new. All of the sounds combined with the scents began lulling her into the trance she sought.

The colors grew even brighter, and although she knew it wasn't possible, Kiley felt as though she could see through the thick trees into the heart of the forest. Just outlines of what she sensed. It was a bond to the land that allowed her to put a picture to the sounds. Kiley set her cup down on the grass before flopping onto her back. She kept her eyes closed, the world moving around her. It represented everything she'd been searching for. Running her hand along the soft blades of grass brought the realization she could, indeed, bond with the land there.

She didn't know how long she lay there, communing with nature, before she became aware of another presence. Kiley opened her eyes then swung her head to smile at Austin, who sat cross-legged a few feet away, drinking his own mug of coffee.

"Did it work?" he asked.

They both knew it had. Kiley nodded, anyway.

"How did it feel?"

"Wonderful," she confessed.

Austin grinned. He turned his gaze toward the tree line. "I'd hoped you try, but I didn't expect it your first morning here." He wasn't looking at her, but Kiley knew she had his full attention.

"I'm worried about the threats from the felines," she said. "Has Colt called with any more information?"

"No, but he will. We both know Cain is going to get what intel he can out of them."

"What's to stop the Pack from being exposed?"

"Me."

Kiley laughed. "Okay."

"I mean it. I won't let anything happen to those under my protection. I'll do whatever I have to in order to protect us."

"That's why I wanted to try to bond with the land. You're going to need help. You have a bigger Pack than you did when you first settled in this territory."

"I do, but—"

"Your Beta is currently protecting the man who will be the face of all shifters," she continued.

"Yes."

"I won't let you or anyone in this Pack get hurt. So, I wanted to see if the territory would accept me."

Austin remained silent for several minutes, so Kiley picked up her mug and took a sip. She barely managed to swallow the now-cold liquid.

"Here." Austin passed her his own coffee.

Their fingers brushed as she accepted his cup.

"You forgot one point on why you did it," he whispered.

Kiley sipped his fresh drink. "What's that?"

"Me."

She raised an eyebrow. "Care to elaborate?"

"Your feelings for me," he clarified.

He was good. Kiley might not want to admit it, but Austin was going to make her talk about it. "Maybe."

"It's okay," he responded quietly. "You don't have to tell me. You're showing me by being here and wanting to protect our Pack."

She stiffened at his words. "I haven't joined your Pack."

"No, but after you fall in love with me, you will."

He sounded so damn certain. "We'll see." She was above denying what they both knew to be true.

"Yes, we will." Austin rolled to his knees then stood. When he offered his hand to her, she slipped her palm into his. He pulled until she stood on her feet and pressed up against him. "My inner circle will be arriving soon. We should get dressed."

"Okay," she agreed, amused. Austin tried to hide the elation he felt, but she could easily pick up on his emotions. He was happy—delighted—by their talk. "Let's get dressed, then decide how we're going to protect this Pack."

He linked their fingers together after picking up her mug. Oh, the sweetness of walking hand-in-hand, back to the house. This might be her home if she accepted what Austin offered. She wanted to. Being here was so different from being in her home territory. The strands that connected her to her people had long ago disappeared. She didn't love them. But new ones had formed and Austin had been right. She was in love with him and that would tie her to the rest of the Pack.

Kiley hadn't realized she'd grown chilled until she walked into the warm house. Austin led her to the kitchen, where they put their cups in the sink.

"Why don't you take a hot shower while I make us some breakfast?"

"You cook?" she asked in surprise.

"Enough to get by. It was either Colt and I learn some basics, or driving for over an hour every time we wanted to eat."

"Makes sense," Kiley agreed.

"Ginger also takes pity on us. She loves to bake and we usually have some kind of goodies from her."

Kiley laughed. "I can pour a mean bowl of cereal."

"Sounds good," Austin said. "Now, go shower."

"Yes, sir." She gave him a mock salute.

He slapped her ass in retaliation.

"Keep doing that and we'll give your inner circle a show when they get here," she said while wrapping her arms around his shoulders.

Austin immediately slipped his hands to her ass and lifted. Kiley hooked her legs over his hips until she felt his erection against her. She humped, causing Austin to stumble until her back hit the wall.

"Yes!" she hissed when he thrust his cock against her. "I need."

"Me, too," he grumbled.

He moved fast. Austin let her legs go, but the instant her feet touched the floor, he spun her around. Kiley barely had time to get her hands in front of her to keep her face from hitting as he pushed her against the hard surface.

"Hurry." She was desperate to have him inside her.

Austin yanked down her pajama bottoms, collecting her panties along with them. She arched her back, keeping contact with the denim of his jeans.

"Hold on," he ordered.

Kiley felt him brush his hand against her, undoing his pants before pushing them roughly down his legs. Then Austin was right there behind her, holding his cock as he positioned himself at her pussy.

"Please," she sobbed with need.

He pushed in with one long, smooth stroke. Kiley reached behind her and gripped his hip to keep him from drawing out again, wanting to savor the feeling of fullness.

"You okay?" he whispered in her ear.

"Perfect." Kiley dropped her head onto his shoulder.

"Mine," he said roughly. He brought his hand around to rest it at the base of her neck. He tightened his fingers around her neck and instead of fear, arousal shot through her.

She couldn't help squirming.

"Like that?"

"Yes."

Austin began a lazy thrust and withdrawal while keeping his hand in place. Kiley sensed a connection to him in a way she'd never experienced before. She'd swear she felt every beat of his heart.

Emotions flooded her until Kiley grew overwhelmed. Austin took her past where she'd ever thought was possible. His cock filled her again and again, slow and steady at first, until she clawed at the wall, screaming at him for more.

She orgasmed so hard her knees went week. Austin let go of her neck to catch her around the waist. He held her upright as he plunged deep until he, too, climaxed.

The ground rushed up to meet her fall, but instead of landing, Austin's body was between her and the hard floor. Kiley rested her head on his chest as they lay on the tiles, trying to recover.

Austin wanted nothing more than to savor having Kiley in his arms. What they'd experienced was indescribable. She'd given in to him fully, allowing him to control every part of her. Power and adrenaline coursed through him and he knew it was because of Kiley.

"I didn't hurt you, did I?"

She laughed. "Not at all. I feel wonderful."

Well, that was a ringing endorsement if he'd ever heard one. "We'd better hurry if we don't want to be discovered by my inner circle. Ginger should be walking in at any minute."

"Ugh." She rolled off him until she was on her hands and knees by his side. "She probably doesn't even knock."

"Nope." He grinned, folding his arms behind his head. He didn't miss the once-over she gave him. Austin had barely gotten his jeans to his knees before he'd had to be inside her. Now his pants were uncomfortably twisted around his body and the tile was cold against his ass.

"Keep lying there all cocky," Kiley said with a frown. "Show your Pack your best assets."

He laughed. "I forgot how much you don't like when others see me naked."

She huffed, climbing to her feet. "Yeah, yeah, yeah. Keep making jokes."

Austin watched her sauntering out of the room. Only after he'd heard the bedroom door close did he climb to his feet. As he straightened his clothes and got them refastened, the back door opened.

"Is it safe to come in?" Ginger called.

Austin strolled to the sink and washed his hands. "Yes."

The sliding glass door closed with footsteps heading in his direction.

"It smells like sex in here," Ginger said, joining him.

"I'm sure it does." He refused to be embarrassed, even if it had been his sister who had almost caught him and Kiley passed out on the floor.

"Are you marking your territory?" she asked quietly.

Austin shut off the tabs of the faucet. Had he been? That hadn't been his intention. However, now Ginger had brought up the subject, he had to admit he wouldn't mind if his inner circle realized he'd laid a claim to Kiley. They might not be mated, but Kiley was his.

Ginger placed her hand on his shoulder and leaned in to him. "I'm so happy for you," she whispered.

He grabbed one of the towels off a rack and dried his hands, then pulled his sister into his arms. They'd been a team, the two of them, for a long time. She would always be there for him, but he wanted to make sure she understood he felt the same way. Austin placed a kiss on the top of her head. "Have I told you lately that I love you?"

She squeezed him hard. "Of course you have."

"I couldn't take care of this Pack without you." He grasped her shoulders to push her back enough to peer down at her. "You do so much more than you have to."

Ginger shook her head. "I was there. In Riker's territory, when those girls were attacked and the Packs got together to discuss how to figure out the party responsible."

"I know," he tried to soothe her.

"I could have found Kiley or helped the Pack then. Being around Riker felt plain wrong, but I didn't see what he was doing," Ginger said. "I failed them."

"You didn't," he reassured her. "I'd heard rumors for years about how bad Riker was, but I never asked any questions or brought it up to the Council. Tyler didn't, either. Instead of looking out for all shifters, I only worried about my Pack. I could have saved Kiley and the others, too."

"Cain was there."

Austin looked up and Ginger spun around to where Kiley stood in the doorway. "What?" he asked.

Kiley shrugged. "I was pointing out that Cain also attended the same meeting Ginger did. So did Cain's best friend, Adam White, who is also an Alpha now. Should I blame them?"

"No," Austin responded, knowing where she was going

with her comments.

Kiley strode forward until she stood in front of his sister. "Ginger?"

"I know it's silly," Ginger said. "I just feel I'd have saved all of you months of torment."

"It's not your fault," Kiley told Ginger. "It's not anyone's fault, except for Riker and his men who hurt us."

Ginger nodded but didn't seem too satisfied.

"Adam's White new Enforcer is Riker's old Enforcer. Larry spent years stepping in front of other members of the Pack, so he took the brunt of Riker's anger. If you don't believe me that there was nothing you could have done, talk to him. He's one of the bravest, kindest men who I know and he's had a hard time moving past what happened. But he did what he could. Just like you didn't know what was happening and cannot take the blame onto yourself. If you try, you'll fall apart, and that's not going to help anyone right now."

Ginger glanced over her shoulder at him before turning to Kiley and grabbing her into a fierce hug.

That was what they needed from Kiley. She would be able to not only help her old Pack mates, but also show his Pack what the newest members could do to assist in everyone's healing.

Ginger laughed, pushing Kiley away. "Okay," she said. "Enough of that talk. We have to get ready for the meeting."

Austin stepped around his sister to address Kiley. "I thought you were going to shower?"

"I am," Kiley responded. "I couldn't find any towels."

"I'll show you." Ginger linked arms with Kiley and led her from the kitchen.

Austin knew he was grinning but didn't even care. His sister and lover were getting along famously. He couldn't have hoped for a better interaction between them. Austin went about making a fresh pot of coffee. Once he had it brewing, he pulled out eggs, bacon, sausage and a can of biscuits.

Breakfast was his favorite meal and he longed to cook for Kiley. Other than grilling out, he also didn't make any other food. But he knew he'd be able to impress her this once and he planned to make a spread that would have her drooling.

He hummed, pulling out skillets and pans. Ginger joined him and took over making the biscuits as he cracked eggs.

It took fifteen minutes for Austin to set the dishes on the table. He'd heard the shower turn off and knew Kiley would be down soon, just as the first of his inner circle arrived. He'd made enough for everyone so they could discuss their plans while they ate.

"Brick is here," Austin said, sensing his head guard on the porch.

The loud banging came less than a minute later.

"I bet Sophie and John are with him," Ginger said. "I'll go let them in."

Ginger started out of the room, but Austin heard the front door open before she was gone. Austin threw down the towel he held and ran forward. He rushed past Ginger in time to see Brick go flying through the living room. His head guard landed with a loud crash and grunt.

"Shit!" Sophie ran to the side of her six-foot-two, two-hundred-and-fifty-pound mate.

Austin stared at Kiley in shock.

She still crouched in a defensive position. Austin shook his head then stalked forward to gather her up.

"Are you okay?" he asked her.

Kiley nodded.

"I'm okay, too," Brick called from the floor where Sophie was helping him sit up. "If anyone cares."

"You probably shouldn't have tried to grab the new chick," John said, entering the house then closing the door behind him.

"I was excited!" Brick said.

"You really should have known better," Sophie told Brick, rubbing his back.

"Did I miss something?" Kiley whispered. "Why did the

big guy try to grab me?"

"I knew your mom," Brick said. "She was my aunt's best friend."

"Oh." Kiley glanced up at Austin, frowning. "Sorry."

Austin didn't really know how to respond. Kiley had taken down his most experienced guard and wasn't even out of breath.

"You've got to show me that move," Ginger said.

"Me, too!" Sophie agreed.

Kiley grinned. "Sure."

"Well." Austin waved his hand. "If Brick can get up, why don't we go into the kitchen and eat some of the food I've been slaving away making for you all?"

John snorted. "Since you usually only provide us with a cup of coffee, I'm inclined to think the food isn't to impress us."

Austin smacked John playfully in the back of the head as he escorted Kiley to the kitchen. John laughed before following. Ginger was ahead of them and sat in her usual seat. It wasn't long until Brick and Sophie joined them.

"Here." Austin pulled out a chair for Kiley. "Let me introduce everyone. You met Brick, who is the head guard and in charge of all the security for the Pack. His mate, Sophie, is in charge of education and has a Masters in early childhood development that helps us care for the pups. John here is the Pack doctor."

Kiley nodded to each person as Austin said their names. He couldn't keep the pride from his voice in speaking about his inner circle. Every Alpha had the choice in who he wanted in the most trusted positions and what skills he required. Austin was lucky enough to be surrounded by loyal and trustworthy people.

"Let's eat and we can talk about how we're going to look after our Pack," Austin said.

Brick was the first one to grab a spoon. He scooped up eggs and put them on Sophie's plate, then served himself three times the amount he'd given her. The huge, blond, buff guard didn't look like the perfect match for the five-foot-three, black-haired beauty, but Brick and Sophie had been together over ten years and had twin boys. They were the happiest couple in the Pack, if Austin was any judge. Austin had a strong desire to have the same type of relationship and he prayed he wouldn't be disappointed.

Austin helped Kiley fill her plate and he waited until everyone had settled down before he spoke. "Colt hasn't called back yet, but I expect to hear from him soon. Cain will get everything he can out of the felines. I spoke to our Council representative and he offered any help we might need."

"Are they going to come after you?" Sophie asked.

"I don't think so," Austin said. "From what Colt has gathered, the felines are trying to stop us from announcing our presence to the humans. Since I've already declined, the Council thinks this group will target those who agree to go public. We should be safe."

"Do you really believe that?" Brick asked.

"I don't know, but we're not going to risk it. From now on, we'll have full shifts of guards," Austin said. "Rotate them as much as you can to keep them fresh."

"That would be easier to do if we had a wall or some gates. I don't like you being so exposed."

It was a familiar argument between them. Colt had agreed with Brick, but so far Austin had been able to avoid giving in. The threat of the felines had him rethinking his position, though. "I know," Austin said. "But we need to plan around that."

"You'll finally consider it?" Brick pressed.

Austin glanced over at Kiley. He knew she liked that they weren't surrounded by walls and held in. Being able to offer that freedom to her when she'd bonded with the land was so important to him. But he also wouldn't have her in danger. "I'm considering it, but I want to talk to the rest of the Pack."

Brick nodded. "In the meantime, you should stay inside

unless one of the guards is with you. I put them on high alert last night, but they've been keeping their distance to give you privacy."

"I'm not going to pull a guard from duty just because I feel like a walk," Austin argued. "I can handle myself."

"That's not the point," Brick growled. "If anything happens to you, we're all in danger. We have to keep you safe."

Austin linked his fingers with Kiley's and grinned. "Since my lover just put you on your ass, I think the two of us can handle anything that might happen at this house. I'm more concerned about the Pack members who don't have our training."

Brick sighed, peering over at Sophie. "We have to protect the kids first."

"Yes," Sophie agreed.

Austin's cell rang and he dug it out of his pocket. Colt's name and picture flashed on the screen. "It's Colt. Let me see what he can tell us." He rose from the table as he answered, "Hey, Colt."

"Is everything okay there?" Colt asked quickly.

"Yes," Austin assured his Beta. "I have the inner circle here and we're making plans for keeping everyone safe."

Colt's long, deep breath came over the line clearly.

He strolled to the living room and sat on the big leather couch. "What's wrong?" Austin asked.

"Tony heard from Cain. He's getting more information from the felines, especially the youngest one, who didn't even want to be involved."

"Anything we need to know?" Austin questioned.

"Yes, but first we have a bigger problem."

Dread made Austin's stomach clench. "What?"

"The feline Prince is missing," Colt said. "We think he's been kidnapped."

"Kidnapped?" Austin repeated in disbelief. "Wasn't he under guard?" How did the felines let this happen? A Prince of a species would be even more important than an

Alpha!

"They believe the guard might have been involved."

"They?" Austin asked. "Who is Tony talking to on the feline's side?"

"I'm not really sure," Colt said. "The entire thing is a fucking mess. Tony wants to go help look for the Prince, but his father is forbidding it."

"What do you think?" Austin asked gently. He knew there was more bothering Colt.

"I can see both points of view. If whoever took the Prince got their hands on Tony, it would be devastating. The wolves and felines are sort of leading the charge in going public. We can't let anything happen to Tony. But Tony feels responsible for the Prince, since he's the one who brought him in," Colt explained.

"And you're fighting with Tony about this?" Austin asked, even though he already knew.

"Yeah. He's pretty pissed at me."

"Do whatever you can to keep him safe."

"Oh, I will, whether he wants me to or not," Colt said confidently. "First, I wanted to make sure you and our Pack are safe."

"I promise," Austin said. He peered through the doorway where Kiley and his Pack were still talking. "I'm going to call the Pack together this afternoon and warn everyone. After that, we'll lock down the territory, and we're already putting all the guards on duty. We're safe here, you take care of things there. Is there anything I can do?"

"Not right now. Only stay safe for me. I hate not being able to be with you, but I can't leave Tony now. I don't see him listening to his dad much longer."

"Don't worry about us," Austin said. "Concentrate on what you have to there."

"Thanks."

At least Colt sounded a little better than he had when Austin had first answered the phone. Colt didn't deal well with stress and always wanted to be able to fix things. It would be interesting to see how Colt and Tony's relationship evolved. Austin wanted Colt to be happy and he knew that would be with Tony. Which also meant he'd be losing his Beta soon. That was something he'd have to think about later, though.

"What about the Prince?" Austin asked. "Are we doing anything to help?"

"Yes, the Council is sending some representatives out and Tyler already has Gray helping. Hopefully, that will keep Tony from insisting on joining the search."

"Well, let me know if I can do anything."

"I will," Colt replied. "Tony just walked into the room, so I have to go. I'll call and update you when I know more."

"Sounds good."

Colt disconnected and Austin stared at the phone in his hand. He hated Colt being on his own. They always had each other's backs, but for the first time, their needs were completely different. Colt's place was at Tony's side, trying to help in any way possible. Austin had a Pack to take care of. He also would not have Kiley in any kind of danger. She'd already been through so much and it was time she started to enjoy life.

He was glad he'd already decided not to take his Pack public. When he'd given his decision to Tony and the Council, they'd been understanding and kind. Austin had still felt some guilt, though. He understood why it was important to let the world know they existed and manage the information, but Austin suspected there would be a lot of fear and panic from humans. His territory would be a welcoming retreat from the pressures once the time to become public grew closer. A safe haven. And Kiley would be with him. She'd already bonded with the land, so now he only had to work on getting her to admit that she was falling in love with him. Just as he was with her.

Austin rose from the couch before strolling toward the kitchen. He still couldn't believe the woman he'd been searching for after their one-night stand sat at his table, talking to his sister and the other shifters he was closest to. He'd known after he'd made love to her that she was meant for him. Both his human and wolf had felt the connection. He'd been looking so hard for her, certain she'd be the one to complete him. Kiley was going to be his mate. He needed to convince her of that fact.

"Everything okay?" Ginger asked, rejoining them.

"Not really," Austin said. "The feline Prince has been kidnapped."

Gasps and surprised sounds echoed around the room.

"I want to gather the Pack," Austin said. "They need to know what is going on and I want everyone keeping an eye out. We're going on lockdown."

"I'll call a meeting," Brick told him.

"Let's make it early afternoon," Austin said. He glanced at Kiley. "We'll have a barbecue and have them meet Kiley, as well."

"Uh…" Kiley rubbed her arms. "We don't have to do that."

"We do," Austin responded. "Even with all this going on, we need to make it a priority for the Pack to come together. We have to be strong when the shifters go public."

"I agree," Ginger said and the others were nodding. "We'll eat, introduce you and let them know about the threat. Going on lockdown will keep everyone close, too, so this will be a good time if anyone does want to talk."

Kiley sighed. "Okay, I guess it's best sooner than later."

Austin walked behind her chair and gripped her shoulders gently. "You'll do great. I think this is really going to help finish the healing process."

"I hope so." Kiley peered up at him. "I really do."

Chapter Nine

The backyard bustled with members of the Pack and Kiley couldn't believe the warm reception she was receiving. Even more shocking was how many of her old Pack who had embraced her. Kiley hadn't been close to her parents, especially not after her dad had sold her to Riker and he and her mom had lived the high life before they were killed in a car accident. But the people who came up to her didn't talk about her parents—instead they shared stories about her grandparents from her mother's side.

Kiley felt overwhelmed by the many claims of how much her grandparents had loved her. She'd only been two years old when her grandfather had passed from a heart attack. Less than twelve months later, Kiley's grandma had followed her mate into death. Kiley wished she remembered any family who might have actually loved her, but she'd been too young. Still, that wasn't as hard as hearing apology after apology about not knowing what she'd been going through with Riker. Kiley hated that what had been done to her was still affecting people. She vowed to show the Pack they were strong enough to move on from the past and they were all going to live happily.

Spotting Austin making his way to her, Kiley excused herself from another female and met him halfway across the yard.

"You doing okay?" he asked softly while passing her over a cold bottle of water.

"Yeah." She twisted off the cap and took a long pull before leaning against his side. "It's hard hearing some of the stories about my family, but it's good, too."

Austin brushed his lips against her temple, wrapping his arm around her waist. "There's someone else who wants to talk to you, but she doesn't want to do it in front of everyone else."

Kiley stiffened without meaning to. "Who is it?" She couldn't help but be suspicious.

"She's one of the first who joined my Pack," Austin said. "She's very quiet and I haven't been able to get her to open up with me. I think you'll want some privacy, too."

"Okay," Kiley rolled her shoulders then took a deep breath. Austin wasn't going to give her a name and that bothered her, but Kiley was a big girl. "Where is she?"

"My office."

Kiley took a step forward, but Austin tightened his arm.

"Hey, don't be mad," he told her.

"I'm not mad," she replied.

He merely lifted an eyebrow.

"Much," she amended.

"Trust me." He drew her in close.

Like every other time, her body responded to his nearness. The press of him against her also helped to calm her. "Sorry," she said quietly. "I guess I'm just wound up tight."

"I know." He ran his palm down her spine. "I promise, when everyone leaves, I'm going to pamper you. We'll enjoy a long, hot bath together before I take you to bed and love every inch of you."

Kiley hummed. "That sounds heavenly to me."

"Come on then." Austin threaded his fingers through hers and gave her a little tug.

People smiled at them when they passed. *Well, guess there's no hiding the relationship.* Probably something she should have thought about or spoken to Austin about earlier. Too late now.

Ginger was stepping out of the sliding glass door with Sophie behind her as Kiley and Austin reached the back deck. They passed each other and Ginger reached out and squeezed her elbow before continuing. Kiley knew she was lucky to find Austin's sister so accepting.

In Kiley's opinion, she wasn't good enough to be with an Alpha. If her Rogue status wasn't enough to keep her separate, Kiley also had issue after issue that stopped her from opening up to people. Yes, she was working on it, but a mate to an Alpha needed to be solid.

She missed a step as her thoughts caught up with her. *Mate? Where in the hell did that come from?* She was nowhere near ready for that level of commitment. A wolf mate was for life.

"Hey!" Austin caught her around the shoulders to pull her to a stop. "Look, she wanted to surprise you, but if you're upset—"

"No!" Kiley waved him off. "I was thinking and surprised myself."

"What were you thinking about?"

Of course he would ask. Kiley could lie, but she really didn't want to. She actually wanted to know what he thought about the subject. Did Austin see them being together like that? She knew he wanted her, but did that mean mating? Kiley moved to brace herself against the wall.

"What is it?" Austin asked, concern clearly written on his face.

"What's going on between us?"

He blinked at her several times before he grinned brightly. "We're falling in love."

"Huh?" Kiley hadn't expected that answer.

Austin chuckled. "You heard me. And by the way you're blushing, I don't think this really comes as a shock to you. What do *you* think is going on between us?"

"I don't know," she said. "I mean we're...dating...or maybe not dating but..."

He stepped up and slid his arm around her waist, pulling her close. Kiley peered into his warm gaze.

"We're partners," he told her. "Together, we're going to protect this Pack and help them grow and be happy. Eventually, we will mate and start a family."

"Family?" *Oh, shit, oh, shit, oh, shit!*

"Yes," he said. "A family. Maybe not in a year, or even five years from now, but one day, I want a little girl or boy running around with your eyes and fearlessness."

Wow, Kiley could even picture that. Well, actually she'd love a little boy with Austin's coloring. A little man who would love her and call her mama. She found herself nodding, unable to speak.

"I was giving you time," he told her quietly. "I know you're not ready yet, but since you brought it up, you should know I plan to make you happy for the rest of our lives."

"I don't know why you'd even want me, but I'm not going to question it."

"Good, don't." Austin leaned in and kissed her. Hard.

Kiley wrapped her arms around his neck, pressing her chest against his. Mmm, she loved the taste of him.

"We can't do this now," Austin said, panting, after pulling away.

Oh, yeah, she was supposed to meeting some mystery person. "Later," she told him.

"I can't wait."

After he stepped away, Kiley straightened her clothes to try to gather herself. Austin shifted his erection in his jeans and she wanted to reach out and help him, but that wouldn't get them alone any sooner. Instead, she faced Austin's closed office door.

She strolled forward, feeling it when he stepped behind her. The hall seemed to lengthen with every stride she took down it. Kiley knew that was just her nerves about whatever surprise lay in store for her. As she reached the thick, wooden door, she picked up a recent scent, one vaguely familiar. She couldn't place it. When Kiley paused, Austin leaned against her back while reaching around and turning the knob.

At first, she didn't see anyone. The curtains were open in the large room, allowing the waning light to creep in.

Only the lamp on the desk helped illuminate the space. Movement in the corner of her room had Kiley snapping her head in that direction and she gasped.

"Allison?" she whispered.

"I was afraid you wouldn't remember me."

"Of course I do," Kiley told her. She wanted to rush across the room and embrace her oldest friend, but her feet didn't seem to be working.

Allison smiled while walking forward. "I...can. I... I want to hug you."

Kiley was already nodding. That seemed to be all Allison needed. Allison ran across the room, her long blonde hair flowing behind her, until she launched herself into Kiley's arms. The impact had Kiley grunting and almost falling, but Austin's solid body kept her upright. Allison sobbed into her shoulder and Kiley wasn't sure what to do. It had been so long since she'd seen her childhood friend. Kiley ran her hand over hair and shoulders while murmuring to her.

Finally, Allison pulled back. Kiley wiped the tears from her friend's face. "Hey, what's all this?" she asked gently.

"I..." Allison sobbed. "I'm so sorry I left you."

"Oh, no!" Kiley hugged her tightly before she ushered her to the black leather couch that faced the window. The door clicked closed behind her then Austin's soft footsteps crossed to the other side of the room. Kiley didn't take her attention from her friend, though. Once they reached the couch, Kiley helped Allison sit down before she lowered herself and gripped Allison's hand.

"I can't believe you're here," Allison said, in awe.

"You?" Kiley said with a laugh. "I didn't even know you'd joined Austin's Pack."

"After we left Riker's Pack, my parents didn't really want anything to do with another Pack, but they also didn't want to be Rogue. So, after we traveled around the United States for about a year, we moved to Australia."

"Wow." Kiley was impressed. She'd never gotten to

travel. For Allison to have grown up in another country was amazing to her.

"It was great," Allison told her. "But I never forgot about you. I wish I'd been there for you."

"It's okay," Kiley soothed.

"No, it's not!" Allison wailed. "I've heard the stories about what Riker did to you."

"There's nothing you could have done," Kiley assured her.

"That's the thing, though," Allison said, gripping her fingers. "Do you know why we left?"

"No," Kiley admitted. They'd been so young and she hadn't understood why Allison and her family had disappeared. One day her best friend had been there and the next the house had stood empty and she hadn't been allowed to even speak Allison's name.

"Riker hit on my mom and told my dad he was going to take my mom away from him," Allison said. "My dad knew he wasn't strong enough to fight the Alpha, so in the middle of the night, we packed up everything we could and snuck out of the territory. I begged my parents not to take me away. I didn't understand what was going on."

"There is no way you'd have known." She looked up when Austin walked over and handed them two glasses with a brown liquid. She took a sniff of the strong whiskey and smiled up at him.

Allison took a sip and that seemed to settle her somewhat. She released Kiley's hand and sat back. "Thanks. I needed this."

"Of course," Austin replied softly. He sat in a leather chair across from them.

Kiley was glad he was sticking close. Despite her pleasure at seeing her old friend once again, this was all taking a lot out of her. She was becoming emotionally drained.

"You don't have to do this now," Kiley told Allison.

Allison nodded. "I'd really like to. We're part of the same Pack again. That has to be a sign or something."

Kiley smiled. "I guess you're right." She didn't correct Allison's statement about being part of the same Pack. If Austin was serious about what he'd said earlier, and she had no reason to think he wasn't, she would be joining Austin's Pack. It was only a matter of time.

"I want to get this out of the way so we can start catching up on the good times. We don't have to talk about this again," Allison said.

"I agree," Kiley said. She was getting an opportunity she'd never expected. Allison had been the girl who Kiley had spent hours and hours playing and growing up with. From dolls to learning about their wolf sides, the two had done everything together. Before Allison had left one night and Kiley had never heard from her again.

"My parents didn't ever tell me about why we'd left. At first, I asked and wanted to go home, but as time passed I loved where we lived and our new Pack. It wasn't until after I'd gone to university and was thinking about moving back to the States that they told me what had happened. My mom cried the whole time and my dad was visibly upset. I swore to them that when I returned to the states, I would stay far clear of Riker. I settled in Florida and started my life, but I kept thinking about you and where you might be. I really thought that since we'd gotten out, so did you and your family."

Kiley understood why Allison might think that. If she hadn't actually gone through what had happened to her, it would seem farfetched.

"After a year, I was dying to find out where you were," Allison said. "I began to research Riker's territory. I read articles and newspapers, hoping to come across your name or something. That's when I found the article about your parents' accident."

"Oh," Kiley said. "I never saw that. I didn't even go to the funeral. Riker already had me."

"That article is why I really started searching for you. There was no mention of you at all. Nothing, and that didn't sit right with me. So, I started to discreetly make inquires. I flew in several times before I finally found a Pack member out in public, but when I asked about you, no one knew much more than that you'd been sent away to boarding school. No city and no one had a clue where you'd gone after graduation. It didn't make sense to me."

"You never did not like getting answers," Kiley commented.

"Even less now," Allison said with a smile. "I was still trying to figure out my next move when Riker was taken into custody. I still didn't know what had happened to you, and then my dad got sick. I had to return home to care for him."

"Oh, I'm so sorry to hear that." It might have been several years, but she remembered Allison's parents fondly.

"My dad ended up passing away, and a month later my mom did, too," Allison said. "By the time I returned to the States, the entire territory was a mess and there was a new Alpha. The rumors about what you'd been through had gotten out and guilt ate me up. Instead of continuing my search, I chickened out and joined some of the other Pack members who came here."

"I'm glad you did," Kiley said sincerely. "You can't blame yourself. There is no telling what would have happened to you if Riker had learned what you were up to. I'm glad you didn't get caught."

"Even after Riker had gone, I was still scared. I thought you must hate me."

"No." Kiley pressed Allison's hand between hers. "Believe it or not, other people tried to help. They usually disappeared. I couldn't live with myself if that had happened to you." She glanced over at Austin before turning her attention once more to Allison. "I'm glad you ended up here."

"Me, too." Allison glanced between her and Austin as well. "I'm glad we both did. So, do you think we can hang out again?"

Kiley suddenly grew emotional. It had been barely over twenty-four hours and her life had completely changed. She'd found a territory she felt she belonged to. She also had a chance of having a family again. Austin wanted her and Ginger was already teasing her about being sisters. Now her oldest friend had come back into her life. It was so unbelievable. "Yes," she managed.

"Thank you," Allison whispered, hugging her tightly.

Kiley returned the embrace but had to pull away. She'd started to shake and needed a few minutes alone.

Austin rose, then reached for her. "Why don't I show Allison out and break up the gathering? I've already spoken to everyone and they know to be careful and watch out for anything suspicious. I think we can end the party."

"Sounds good," she said, turning to stare out of the window. Several women had already started to clean up, so she didn't feel guilty about Austin sending everyone home.

The door clicked closed and Kiley knew she was alone. She took a deep breath, but instead of it calming her, Kiley gasped. Tears fell and she collapsed onto the couch. Kiley pulled her legs up and wrapped her arms around them to bury her face.

Now that everything seemed to be coming together, Kiley didn't know what to do. All she wanted was for Austin to come back and hold her. A small part of her was actually scared all of this was too good to be true. If she trusted what was happening and it was yanked away from her, Kiley didn't think she'd survive.

Austin was impatient to get everyone out of his house so he could return to Kiley. Ginger peered over at him and frowned.

"What's going on?"

"Nothing," he assured her. "I think Kiley is overwhelmed. I want to check on her."

"Well, go. I can handle this," Ginger told him.

He glanced around and noticed only a few people

remained. He spotted Brick and waved him over.

"What's up?" Brick asked when he joined them.

"All the guards in place?" Austin asked.

"Yes, sir," Brick said. "Schedule is posted and we're covered. No one is going to get to our Pack."

"Good," Austin praised. "Will you help finish up here then make sure Ginger gets home safely?"

"Really?" Ginger asked.

Austin shook his head. "Please. I need to get back to Kiley, but I also need to make sure you're safe."

"Fine," Ginger agreed. "Now go see to your woman."

Austin was already heading in that direction. He'd hated to leave Kiley at all, but he knew she had needed time by herself. He was halfway across the living room when his cell rang. With a growl, he pulled his phone from his back pocket. Damn, it was Colt, so he had to take the call. "Hello?"

"Hey, Austin," Colt said. "How're things going?"

"Good," Austin assured him. "We're finishing up a Pack get-together so everyone knows to keep an eye out."

"That's great. I spoke to Cain and he doesn't think you're on anyone's radar. The felines confessed they were following Tony. They only went after you and Kiley to scare Tony."

Relief flooded Austin. He wouldn't lower the lockdown or lessen the guards yet, but some of the stress left his body. He hadn't really thought his Pack was at risk, but he couldn't be sure. "That's good. Has he gotten any more information from them?"

"They gave us a name. The Prince's own family is responsible. They don't want to go public and couldn't get the Prince to change his mind. They were attempting to scare us and when that didn't work, they went after the Prince."

"Shit." It was unbelievable that shifters would kidnap their own leader. "Have they found him?"

"No, not yet," Colt said. "The Council representatives

arrived and they'll take the felines to the Council and help with the search. Right now, there isn't much we can do but hope they find him safe, and soon."

"So, you're staying there in Tony's territory?" Austin asked.

"Actually," Colt said, "the Council wants Tony to go to California and I don't think he should go alone. That's a long trip for him to be without a guard."

"I agree," Austin said. "You should go with him."

"Only if you don't need me there."

"We're okay," Austin said. "Tony needs you."

"You're still my Alpha."

"I am. And I'll always be your best friend."

Colt cleared his throat. "Yeah."

Austin knew his Beta struggled with the realization his life was changing. The same as Kiley. He would offer the same advice he planned to give Kiley. "You need to follow your heart. Trust your instincts."

"I know," Colt said quietly. "It's just not easy to do."

He chuckled. "It usually isn't."

"I'll talk to Tony and let you know what our plans are. Maybe after we're done in California, we can come back there. Tony still needs to meet with the other Alpha in Colorado, so we'll be in the area."

"I'd like that."

"You haven't given my room away, have you?" Colt joked.

"Of course not. And it will always be your room, even if you are never here."

"Thanks, man."

"You're welcome," Austin responded seriously. "I'll talk to you soon."

"Okay, bye."

Austin sat for several moments, just enjoying knowing they were really safe. It would still be rough and stressful until the shifters came out and they knew for sure how humans would react. But Austin had time to prepare and get ready for that. In the meantime, he intended to show Kiley how much she was wanted and needed. He believed they'd already started by bringing her old Pack out to see and speak to her. He'd seen for himself how the newest members of his Pack finally began to open up as they saw for themselves that healing was possible. Kiley represented a strong symbol of hope. If she could rebuild her life, then so could they. It might take more time for everyone to understand Riker was no longer able to hurt them, but Austin was certain they'd get there.

He sprang up and hurried to the office where he'd left Kiley earlier. When he pushed the door open, he expected to see her visibly upset much like he'd left her. Instead, she was reclining on the couch with what looked like a fresh drink in her hand. Austin shut the door behind him.

"You okay?" he asked.

"Yes." She lifted the glass in his direction. "I had myself a good cry and wallowed, then took a deep breath so I can enjoy the changes in my life."

"Really?" He was beyond shocked. Not that he didn't think Kiley shouldn't be happy, but he was surprised. "I guess giving you a minute actually helped."

She laughed. "I did. I was sitting here sobbing and rocking myself and it reminded me of how I felt when Riker had me. I promised myself I would never be a victim again. If I let all this overwhelm me, that is exactly what I'd be doing."

Austin strode over to the couch and sat next to her. She straightened out her legs to lay them over his.

"I think you're amazing."

"I wouldn't go that far."

"No, really," Austin told her. He reached over, took her glass and drank down the rest of the whiskey.

She raised an eyebrow at him. "Thirsty?"

"Celebrating," he corrected. "Colt called and doesn't think there's a real threat to the Pack. We'll keep the extra guards on rotation, but I'm sure we're safe."

"Oh, God!" she said. "That is great!"

"Yeah," Austin agreed. "Even better — Tyler's Pack shouldn't be in danger, either. The felines told Cain it was all just to scare Tony. With Tony out of the territory, there shouldn't be any more problems. Even with his decision to go public when it's time."

Kiley nodded. "Jeez." She placed her hand on her stomach. "I didn't realize how twisted up I was inside until you told me that."

Austin grinned at her. "That's exactly how I felt."

"What else do you feel?" she asked, while running the tip of her finger up the seam of his jeans.

"Well." He wiggled around, stretching to place the glass on an end table. Then he gripped her waist and lifted her until she lay sprawled over his lap. "Let me show you."

Kiley was giggling, but she immediately straddled him, bracing her legs on the couch. She rolled her hips and the friction over his cock caused a grunt to slip out of him.

"Oh, I feel you all right," she teased.

With his hands on her thighs, Austin held her down while pushing up. His cock was so hard and he wanted to be buried deep inside her.

"Shit," she hissed, dropping back her head.

Austin leaned forward, placed his lips over the slim column of her neck and began to kiss and nibble. He could still taste the soap from her shower earlier and the clean scent mixed with her natural flavor on his tongue aroused him further.

"Austin." She panted out his name.

He stood, clutching her in his arms. She scrambled out of his hold to tug at his shirt. Austin yanked it over his head before she grabbed the bottom of her top and removed it as well.

"Get your pants off," she ordered.

"You, too," Austin replied.

It was a race to get naked. He toed off his shoes and bent down to remove his socks. Kiley struggled to get her jeans down her legs, but Austin easily climbed out of his and when he was done, stood aside to watch her until she'd finally removed all her clothes.

Kiley went down on her knees and grasped his cock.

"Baby," he murmured, burying his hand in her hair.

"Just a little taste," she said. Kiley lowered her mouth to his groin. First, she ran her tongue over the slit of his shaft before licking down the side.

It took everything in him not to hold her head still and thrust down her throat. Instead, he gritted his teeth as Kiley licked up the other side of his cock. When she reached the tip once again, this time she did take all of him inside her mouth.

Austin moaned, the warm suction making him draw out the sound. He peered down at her through half-opened eyes and saw what a beautiful picture she made. With her right hand wrapped around the base of his cock, she bobbed her head while staring up at him.

"Touch yourself, too," he demanded. "I want to see."

Very slowly, Kiley trailed her left hand down her own body until she was running her fingers over her clit then out of his view. He could tell the moment she pierced herself, sucking him deeper while humming.

Austin smiled before he placed both hands on her shoulders. He pressed his shaft deeper, then withdrew with care. He did it again, making sure he remained gentle, but slid almost down her throat with each thrust.

She was letting him control the rhythm and that made him feel powerful. He wasn't taking anything from her. Kiley giving herself over to him was amazing. Allowing Austin to be in charge. To have such a strong, wonderful woman kneeling in front of him astonished him. He felt the first warnings that he was going to come and pulled out of her mouth.

"Up," he said, holding out his hand to help her rise.

She withdrew her fingers before climbing to her feet. Austin tugged her into his arms to kiss her. He made love to her mouth like he wanted to do to her body. Kiley rose on tiptoe to tangle her tongue with his. Austin walked her backward until her knees hit the couch and they both went down.

With his lips still against hers, he rubbed his thumb in circles against her clit. She strained against him, spreading her legs wide, panting. Austin ran his thumb through her folds until he felt the wetness of her pussy.

"Please," she cried, after ripping her mouth from his.

Austin lifted up enough so he could grasp his cock and position himself. He pressed inside with one long, smooth move.

Kiley arched as he entered her.

Up on his elbows, he peered down at her while his shaft throbbed inside her. "You're mine," he told her. "Just like I'm yours."

"Yes," she whispered.

That was all he needed to hear. Austin flexed his hips, pushing in before drawing back out. Then he thrust again. He was already so close to coming he knew it wouldn't take him long.

Kiley stroked his back as she rode the waves of ecstasy. It was natural for the speed to pick up and his plunges to gain in strength. They moved in sync, their bodies sliding and grinding against each other's. Austin closed his eyes and bucked and thrust.

She came, yelling out his name, and Austin remained driving forward until he was filling her with his cum. Instincts hit him hard, his wolf restless, as he claimed her in the most basic way.

A little dizzy, he collapsed on top of her and she gasped. He was probably too heavy, but Austin couldn't move just then.

"Promise me you'll do that every night," she murmured against his neck.

"I swear," he told her. "As long as you want me, I'll give you everything I have."

With a little hum of happiness, she nuzzled him.

Austin would keep his vow. He had his Pack. He had his family, friends and everything he could ever want. All he'd been missing was the woman who would complete him. The mate who he had been meant to find. He'd never imagined he'd find that person in a stubborn but caring Rogue, but he had. Kiley was his perfect match and no matter what they faced in the upcoming months with the shifters going public, he knew that together they could weather any storm.

Pack Territory

Excerpt

Chapter One

The wind blew so hard Adam White could feel it rustling his fur even as he stood still. He ignored the strong breeze to remain staring down on his territory. Adam felt the deep connection to the land and knew he'd do anything to bring his Pack back together.

The stress of an attack several months ago that had almost killed one of the female members had finally begun to ease. His father, the Alpha at the time, hadn't recovered and Adam feared he never would. Christian had always been a wonderful father and leader, but Adam had had to step into the position.

Adam was terrified.

Since it wasn't a full moon, Adam didn't have anyone to currently watch over, but he still felt the pressure of knowing every member of the Pack was relying on him in one way or another. He'd barely turned twenty-eight and already he was responsible for so much.

There didn't seem to be any break coming soon. He had some hard decisions to make, the first being a Pack Beta or Enforcer. Every Pack had a second in command. Whether they chose a Beta who would be the liaison between Pack member and Alpha, or an Enforcer who played a more hands-on role as protector remained up to each Alpha. Christian had led with a Beta, but as the man wanted to ready to retire, Adam would need to make up his own mind.

No one knew yet but Adam was leaning more toward having an Enforcer. His best friend, Cain, served as Enforcer for one of the largest Packs and Adam liked the confidence that Pack had in the inner circle. After the attack on Mindy, there had been no question that his Pack needed to feel safe again. Adam truly believed that an Enforcer would benefit them the most.

Adam wanted to have an open door to his Pack. They weren't even a third of the size of Cain's, but the protection of every member would be his top priority. It was going to be hard to tell his father, though. Christian barely came out of his room and only spoke to a few people.

Luckily Christian's oldest friend, Logan, was visiting for a while. Logan currently served as the Beta for the largest Pack in Texas so it was pretty special that Logan and Gage, the Alpha, were giving Logan time to help Christian.

Hopefully there could be help for his father.

Every night when Adam laid down his head, he worried his father would decide to end his existence. It was that fear that kept him from turning to his dad when he needed him the most. He could call Cain, but his best friend was trying to sort out a new relationship and Adam didn't want to bother him. That left him on his own to figure out things. The only other people he stayed close to were Pack. That wasn't to say he wasn't getting assistance from other Alphas or the Council. Adam spent more time on the phone than he'd ever thought he would. Most people had advice or recommendations, but the choice fell to him.

From high on a ridge, he could see the entire expanse of his territory and it filled him. Yes, becoming the Alphas was full of complications, but he wouldn't want anyone else to take over.

The land, people and trouble belonged to him.

He threw back his head and howled. Calling out to his Pack that he stood there watching over them. They were safe.

A few of his Pack must have been in their wolf form as well, since he was greeted by answering cries.

Adam took a step and slowly started his way back home.

The ridge led him into the small forest that they sped through as a Pack on full-moon runs.

Contrary to popular beliefs, they weren't werewolves. They also didn't have to transform during the full moon. Shifters, they could call on the change whenever they wanted. But Adam still loved to run through the woods with the Pack. It was tradition, not a need. He felt the importance of keeping the familiar customs and rituals.

It was cooler under the canopy of the trees, but Adam didn't mind. He'd raced through earlier, tiring himself out so he'd be able to sleep better when he went to bed. The late nights and early mornings were made more difficult because he couldn't sleep.

As he trotted along, he made sure to keep his senses open. The guards were on duty, stationed all around, but Adam knew they couldn't have too many out watching. Until Adam was sure that every member of his Pack was safe, he would continue to double the protection around his territory.

He didn't come across anyone while making his way to the tree where he'd stashed his clothes.

In the old days, he would have walked naked through the house, up to his room, but as the Alpha, he was trying to learn that he wasn't just another Pack member anymore.

His belongings were right where he'd left them and Adam quickly pulled on his faded jeans and T-shirt before picking up his phone. Four missed calls.

Jeez, he'd only been gone an hour.

Adam listened to the voicemails as he headed up the hill to the back door of the Alpha house. His house now.

When he'd turned twenty-one, Adam had moved into a cabin in the territory, but he now lived back in his old room. He loved the space, set up like a small apartment, but it also meant he was constantly surrounded by people.

Nothing too pressing in the calls. One of the members needed to speak to him, his sister was checking in and there were two calls from friends asking when they'd see him. Adam snorted. *Not for a while.* Since they were humans, he couldn't actually tell them what was going on, so he'd used the excuse his dad was sick. Which wasn't a total lie.

Opening the sliding glass door to enter the house, Adam took a deep breath. He smiled at the smell of cakes and cookies. His sister was getting a head-start on the baking for the next day. She always cooked enough food for an army, and his mouth watered in anticipation. If he didn't have the self-control he did, Adam would weigh five hundred pounds. Laura was truly talented in the kitchen. She'd never left the main house, instead staying with their father and now him. Adam hoped she'd meet someone to mate with one day, but he enjoyed having her close.

He took another breath and found the man he was searching for. His father and former Pack Alpha was in his room. Adam wasn't surprised. Hopefully Christian remained in his human form, because the amount of time his father stayed shifted was really worrying him. Adam had tried to talk to his dad, but Christian still carried around so much guilt. Mindy hadn't been the only female hurt in the recent attacks. She had been just the only one from their Pack.

The only person who seemed to be able reach Christian at all was Logan. Adam selfishly hoped Logan wouldn't have to hurry home to his own Alpha any time soon.

Adam thought about stopping by the kitchen to see Laura, but he knew someone was waiting to talk to him, so headed to his office instead.

Opening the door to the Alpha's workplace, Adam then stepped inside and flipped on the light. He had taken his new position only two months before and hadn't changed anything in the office or the house. He didn't know if he even wanted to, though several friends had suggested it would help the transition if he properly claimed the space and made it his own.

Sometimes, Adam still felt as if he were playing dress-up and his father would walk back into the office and demand Adam stop messing around. Intellectually, he knew that wouldn't happen, but he struggled with it daily. The Council, made up of former Alphas who policed the Packs, had given their blessing for him to take over. His Alpha position was official.

While Adam was growing up, his father had always been there for him and had made running the Pack look so easy. Adam had found out there was a lot that went on behind the scenes he'd never known about.

He needed help, and now that he'd decided on an Enforcer instead of a Beta, he needed to figure out who would be best for the role. There wasn't anyone in the Pack he thought fit the bill for what he needed. He would have to bring someone in, which wouldn't be easy. Of course, first he needed to find the man or woman.

Once he'd reached the desk, he turned on the computer and waited for it to boot up. As he did so, he fired off a text to the sentry on duty inside to send in the Pack member who needed to speak to him.

He called out for them to enter when the knock came, but it wasn't until he saw the young woman peek around the male shifter that Adam cursed not having gone to his room and changing first. He was tired and had just wanted to find out how he could help. Of course, the minute he hadn't follow proper procedure, Tasha Johnson would show up.

Adam had been lusting after Tasha for over a year now. The young woman didn't seem to notice him, though. She was raising her teenage sister single-handedly, and as much as the Pack helped, Tasha seemed to prefer to do most things on her own. Which meant she worked a lot and didn't hang around the same party crowd Adam did.

Things were changing, though, so maybe he'd be able to prove to her she could put her trust in him. Not only as an Alpha, but perhaps more. He adjusted his hard-on under the desk before he stood and smiled at her.

Tasha Johnson had followed the guard inside the Alpha house and down the hall. When they'd reached a large oak door, she'd run her sweaty palms over her jeans, as her escort had knocked. She hated to bring her family problems to the new Alpha, but she didn't know where else to turn.

The low voice that had told them to enter sent a shiver down her spine. As the guard had opened the door, then moved out of the way, she'd peeked inside and gotten a good look at the new Pack leader. She'd stayed back at the entrance as Bryan had gone and spoke to the Alpha.

She'd known Adam for years, even though they'd never been close, and had admired him from a distance for a long time now. The fact that she was about to face him alone made her stomach flutter with nerves. He was just so good-looking and she did not want to make a fool of herself in front of him. Plus, she really did need his help.

He'd smiled and liquid arousal had pooled inside her panties. She'd shifted to relieve the pressure, certain if she didn't calm her body, he would be able to tell. A shifter's sense of smell was strong and, as the Alpha bonded more with the Pack, there would be no hiding anything from him.

Her attraction to the Alpha wasn't something she should be worried about, but she couldn't help it. In addition, she really needed to keep her mind off why she was even there. Even just for a minute. She was on the verge of freaking out.

Her entire life had been about showing her younger sister

love and acceptance. Just when Tasha had begun to believe she'd done a good job raising the teen, Crystal had taken off. Now Tasha had to go to the one man she tried to avoid.

When Adam stood and motioned her in, she didn't miss the large bulge trapped in his jeans. The sight of his package did nothing to tame her own desire. Oh, the man just oozed raw sexuality.

The guard left the office without another word and closed the door behind him. The Alpha's scent surrounded her and Tasha struggled not to close her eyes and breathe deeply. She had serious business to discuss.

"Bryan told me that you had a family emergency and needed my help," Adam said as he gestured for her to sit.

Weak-kneed, Tasha gladly took a seat on the worn brown leather couch and clasped her hands in her lap. She should be concentrating on getting her sister back instead of on her desire for a male. Maybe she was a terrible sister, like Crystal had accused her of being. Tears pooled in her eyes, but she refused to let them fall. Even if she were the worst parent figure, Crystal's safety was her first priority. "Yes, Alpha. I need to talk you about my sister, Crystal." *Keep it formal, don't think of him as the man I've been dreaming about. Should be easy enough.*

He sat in the chair across from her and leaned forward. "I'm listening. Whatever you need, I'll help. But call me Adam. There's no need to be so formal."

Well, there goes that plan. Crystal, think about Crystal. Where should I start? "I'm not sure if your father told you about my family when you took over the Pack." She was so nervous she could feel sweat bead on her forehead. She hated talking about her family and sharing the pain of her past.

She saw the sympathy in his eyes when he spoke. "Why don't you tell me?"

Tasha took a deep breath before starting, "Five years ago, my father left our family. I'm still not sure where he went, but my mother didn't take it well. Six months after he left, she ended her existence and left Crystal with me. She was eleven."

He nodded but didn't comment. She appreciated him letting her get the story out quickly. The sooner she finished, the sooner she could once again bury her pain.

"I've tried to do the best I can, but I don't always understand what she is going through. My sister Crystal is a…non-shifter." Tasha waited for his reaction. Being a non-shifter was an embarrassment for her sister. Tasha only saw how wonderful her sibling was instead of whether she could shift or not, and even though she didn't fully understand the issue, she always respected Crystal's wishes. They hadn't told many people, because a lot of Pack members considered non-shifters lower class.

"Go on," he told her gently, and she didn't hear or see anything negative from him.

"Crystal's had a hard time lately with some of the kids from school. That's why I think she ran away." That and she claimed Tasha was trying to keep her away from humans but insisted the both of them attend Pack activities. But Tasha didn't want to get into that right now. She'd only been trying to show Crystal that everyone accepted her, loved her.

"Do you have any idea where she could have gone?" he asked and Tasha just stared at him. Didn't he want to ask questions about the non-shifter part of the story? He didn't say anything more, instead simply waited for her reply.

"I do. I talked to her best friend and she told me that Crystal has been talking to a boy in the city over the Internet. She probably went there." Tasha spoke quickly. "I have his name and number. I keep calling, but no one is answering. He is older and I'm worried about what he might do to her."

Adam leaned over and placed his hand over hers. "Give me the details and I will find her. I promise you that."

Tasha could feel tears threaten to fall in relief. "Thank you, Adam. Thank you."

He squeezed her hand before releasing it. "That is what I

am here for. Do you have the information with you?"

Tasha nodded and dug in her purse for her small notebook. Her hand still tingled from where Adam had touched her. "I wrote it all down." She tore out a page and handed it to him, hoping he didn't notice her hands shaking.

"I'll work on this and keep you in the loop on what I find out," he told her as he stood. "I know realize it's useless to tell you not to worry, but I hope you know you can trust me."

"I do," she assured him. She wasn't lying. Even if Adam hadn't been the Alpha, there was a good chance Christian would have charged his son to handle this, anyway. She wasn't sure who Adam would send, but she understood knew he would keep his word about finding Crystal.

"I'm glad," Adam said. "Why don't you head home in case she calls? Let me know if you hear from her."

She nodded as he held out his hand and helped her to her feet.

An electric current ran between them and she gasped in surprise. Adam seemed stunned for an instant before he grinned at her. That wicked look on his face had Tasha longing to reach out and grab hold of him.

It wasn't just the fact she found him attractive, making her want the strength of his arms around her. She was tired and heartbroken. It was hard raising a teenager, even with help from her friends and adopted family. That was what the Pack meant to her. Honorary aunts, uncles, cousins and more.

"Hey, it's okay," Adam said, pulling her close.

Tasha allowed him to comfort her and it felt so right. He wrapped his strong arms around her shoulders and she buried her face in his chest. This time, she couldn't hold the tears at bay. She sobbed into his shirt and let go of all her worry.

He rubbed her back and murmured, "It's okay. We'll find her. I did some pretty shitty things when I was her age. You raised her well and she knows right from wrong."

Oh, God! She had needed to hear the words.

Once she felt as though she had control again, she patted his chest before pulling away. The expression on his face was so soft and caring she almost started crying again. How had the two of them fought this connection that was so obvious?

"I'll walk you out," Adam told her as he stepped away.

"Okay," she agreed.

He placed his hand on her lower back and she jolted. Yes, the attraction was there and strong. They didn't speak as they left the office and strolled down the hall toward the front door. Tasha noticed that nothing had been changed inside the Alpha house and she was surprised. It was quite normal for a new Alpha to at least make small modifications so the Pack accepted the transition of power. It had only been a couple of months since Christian had stepped down, but Adam needed to take control.

Not that Tasha felt she should voice her thoughts just yet. There was always more than what appeared on the surface when it came to Alphas, and if the dark circles under Adam's beautiful eyes were any indication, this new Alpha was struggled with something.

She hated to add to his stress, but some things couldn't be helped. It did comfort her that even if he were going through his own troubles, he was willing to give his time and attention to her needs.

She had no doubt that Adam would make a wonderful Alpha.

He opened the front door for her and she paused to look up at him. "I know that you have other things to worry about—"

"No," he interrupted. "You don't need to concern yourself about that. We concentrate on your sister."

Tasha reached down and gripped his hand. She didn't need to say anything else. Her touch showed her appreciation and since she was barely hanging on to her emotions, it would be best to remain silent.

She released him before walking out of the door then jogging down the stairs. Her old car sat in front of the large Alpha house, standing out as a reminder that she didn't fit in there. She wasn't fancy or knock-out gorgeous. She was kind of plain and men didn't usually pay her too much attention. But she felt his.

The entire time she moved away from him, she could sense his gaze on her. It felt good to hold the interest of such a gorgeous and powerful shifter. If she put a little more wiggle in her hips, who could blame her?

It wasn't until she climbed behind the wheel that she glanced up toward the house. Adam was still there, leaning against the door frame, and his hot gaze bore into her. She shivered. Maybe she would have something to thank her sister for once she'd dragged her hormonal teenage butt back.

Tasha pushed the key in the ignition, then started her car. She'd given the information she had to the Alpha, but that didn't mean that she was going to lay it all at his feet. If she didn't hear from Crystal tonight, she would head into the city herself.

Adam waited until the brake lights on Tasha's car were out of sight before he closed the front door. A missing teenager was not what the Pack needed. Not only was there a chance of the young girl getting really hurt but she belonged to his Pack and he'd vowed to keep them safe.

He turned toward his office to begin researching the name and number that Tasha had provided. She hadn't told him how old the guy who Crystal had been talking to was and Adam wanted as much information as possible.

Halfway to his workspace, he spotted the figure leaning against the wall. Adam frowned and hurried his pace.

"Is my dad okay?" he asked Logan.

"He's fine," Logan assured him. He grinned before clasping Adam on the shoulder. "I did want to talk to you if you have a minute."

"Sure." Adam waved Logan toward his office.

"Everything okay?" Logan asked, walking in front of him.

Adam followed and closed the door behind them. He didn't want anyone else to hear about Pack business. He trusted and respected Logan.

Logan and Christian had been friends Adam's entire life, so even though they'd lived in different Packs, Logan had always been around. He was like an uncle to Adam.

"One of our teenagers took off to the city to meet up with an older boy," Adam told him.

Logan chuckled. "Sometimes I don't know how we make it from about fifteen to nineteen."

Adam nodded his agreement as he headed toward the small bar in the corner of the room. "Drink?"

"Whatever you're having is fine," Logan said.

"Whiskey?" Adam offered.

"Yeah," Logan answered. Instead of sitting, he prowled around while Adam fixed the drinks. Logan might seem fine, but it was obvious to Adam something was on the older shifter's mind.

Adam finished pouring the liquor, then picked up both glasses. He handed one to Logan. "What's up?" He couldn't help but be worried about his dad.

"Let's sit," Logan suggested.

That couldn't be good, but Adam walked toward the couch and sat. Logan joined him. As much as Adam wanted to press Logan, he waited. Finally, after Logan had taken a sip, he sighed before setting his drink on the table.

"I have to return home," Logan informed him.

Damn, it wasn't half an hour ago that Adam had been hoping Logan would be able to stay a while. "Right away?" Adam asked.

Logan rubbed his hands roughly over his face. "Yeah, my Alpha's mate is pregnant and he's given me as much time as he can, but he needs me back. Gage is worried about security while she's expecting. I have to return to my job."

"I know," Adam said. It hurt, but Logan had already spent so much time with his dad. "I'm just worried about my father."

"He's doing much better," Logan said.

"I don't know," Adam confessed. "He barely talks to me anymore."

"Give him time," Logan said. "He's working through some issues and it's taking him time to get his head on straight. He will, though. He loves you and your sister."

Adam sighed. He appreciated Logan's words, but that didn't mean he could or would stop worrying. "I wish you didn't have to leave."

"That's what I wanted to discuss," Logan said.

Adam snapped his head over to look at him.

"I'd like to ask Christian to come back home with me. It will give him a chance to get away from everything and hopefully settle."

He wanted to say no, scream it, even, but Adam knew Logan was probably right. His dad was going to waste away in his room if he didn't get a change of scenery. Adam was hurt, but Logan was dead-on.

Adam rose and paced to the opposite side of the room. The blinds were open and he could see the backyard. The pool, barbecue and lawn chairs. They'd used to sit out there at night, he and his dad, never talking about much. Just enjoying each other's company and the night coming alive around them. He missed those times. If he didn't give his dad space to heal, he might not ever get back the most important man to him.

"Take him with you," Adam said without turning around.

He didn't hear Logan rise, but he wasn't surprised when a hand clamped down on his shoulder.

"I'll take good care of him," Logan promised.

Adam nodded.

"Can I make another suggestion?" Logan asked quietly.

He turned, smiling. "Sure."

"Maybe it would be a good idea for you to have a break of your own," Logan said.

"I can't just leave," Adam said.

"Your dad left the territory. Went on vacation or visited other Alphas," Logan pointed out.

"He had his inner circle in place," Adam said.

"And until you choose your own, they're still here," Logan pointed out. "Let them help. Yes, most have been in the position so long they're ready to retire, but no one is abandoning you."

"I feel alone," Adam confessed.

"I know," Logan said. "It's one of the things your dad and I argue about. He's proud of you. Damn, boy, your father believes in you. He doesn't see that you still need some guidance."

"What should I do?" Adam asked. It was the first time he'd asked anyone that question.

"Go bring your teenage Pack member back," Logan said. "That will help you see what you're fighting for. Connect you to the Pack."

It wasn't a terrible idea. If he left early enough, he might only be gone a day or two. He could rely on his dad's men. Plus, his sister was there, along with the guards. "I might just do that."

"Good." Logan pulled him into a quick hug, then slapped his back. "Good."

As Logan let go of him to head for the exit, Adam was so damn grateful. "Hey, Logan," he called.

Logan turned at the door.

"Thank you."

"Of course." Logan smiled. "You can call me anytime. I'm here for you, too."

Adam let the older shifter go. It was time he made some calls so he could take care of Pack business. In addition, he'd be able to drop in and see Cain. Cain's mate was finishing school and he was currently staying in an apartment not far from the campus.

With a plan forming, Adam headed to his desk to get the ball rolling.

More books from
Crissy Smith

Book one in the Bloodlines series

If trouble doesn't come to him, he'll find it on his own.

Book one in the Were Chronicles series

Marissa Boyd finds herself drawn into a world she can never be a part of, complete with an Alpha wolf who takes whatever he wants. And he wants her.

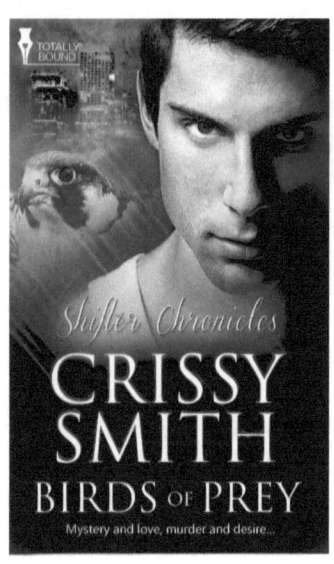

Book one in the Shifter Chronicles series

Mystery and love, murder and desire… It's going to be a rough week for the agents of the Birds of Prey shifter division.

Piper's Happily Ever After
had been postponed...

Designated Alpha

CRISSY SMITH

Part of the What's her Secret? collection

Piper's happily ever after has been postponed. Destiny is funny like that.

About the Author

Crissy Smith

Crissy Smith lives in Texas with her husband, daughter, and three Labrador retrievers. The three dogs love to curl up under her computer desk and nap while she writes. It doesn't leave a lot of room for her but what's a woman to do?

When not writing or reading, she enjoys hunting, camping and shooting. But she has a girly side too and is addicted to pedicures and coffee.

She has been writing since she was a teenager and still loves everything to do with the paranormal. Her stories and characters all have a place in her heart. She loves the alpha male, the dominant werewolf, or the Master vampire which find their way in most of her books.

Learn more about the characters she has created at her website where they have their very own page. It will be updated from time to time to let you know what's going on with them. You can also find out who will be in the next book.

Crissy Smith loves to hear from readers. You can find contact information, website details and an author profile page at https://www.totallybound.com/